PIROUETTE

THE BALLET SERIES
BOOK 3

AMY SHOMSHAK

Pirouette

First Edition | 2025

Albert's Bridge Books

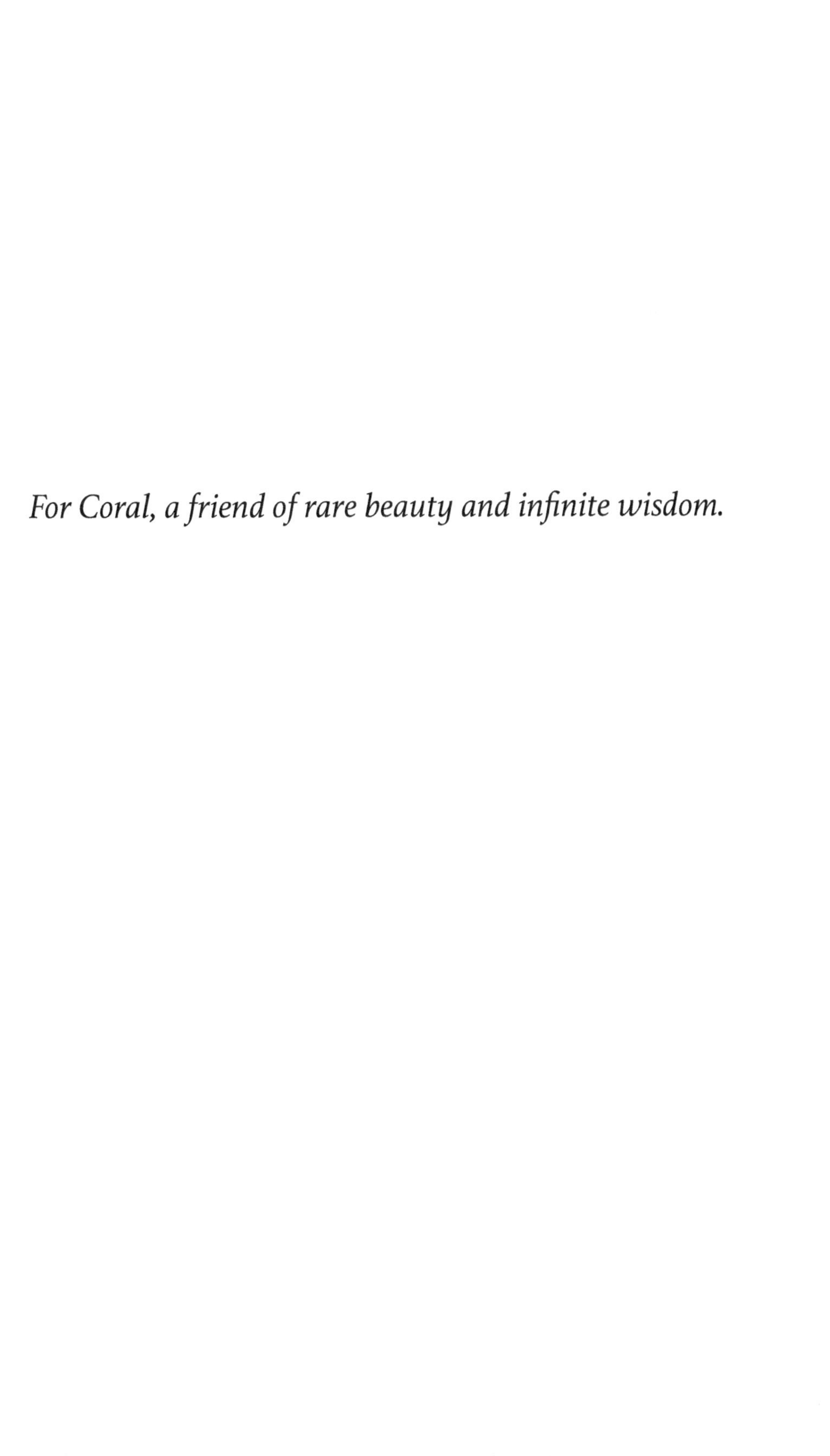

For Coral, a friend of rare beauty and infinite wisdom.

There was a boy, a very strange enchanted boy
  They say he wandered very far, very far
  Over land and sea
  A little shy and sad of eye
  But very wise was he

Eden Ahbez

1

———————

Gina stood next to her mother on a busy corner downtown in Minneapolis. The sun was shining. She felt warm in her sweatshirt and jeans. People crossed back and forth in front of them. Cars and buses rolled by.

Gina's mother, Lily, brushed away a strand of long dark hair that had come loose in the breeze. She pointed up to the dark, red stone building in front of them. "Gina, look at the windows on the fourth floor. Someday you will study ballet there with Madame Branitskaya. She was my teacher."

Gina raised her chin and brushed back her own dark hair. She gazed at the floor to ceiling windows on the fourth floor. There were very high ceilings inside. The building looked frightening.

Gina didn't quite know what to say. She breathed lightly, "But not today? I'm in sixth grade, mom. I'm only ten and a half."

"No, not yet. You are still too young."

She held her mother's hand. Gina felt that she was part of her. Gina was part of Lily's joy, her grace, her sadness. She didn't mind feeling her mother's sadness. As long as she could be part of her mother, Gina had a place in the world. She simply understood that part of her was Lily. That was all.

Several older girls with hair in tight chignons hurried into the building. Pointe shoe ribbons floated out of the tops of their dance bags. One was still pinning up her hair as she followed the others. "Angela, come on!" one of the girls called back. They disappeared into the building.

Gina looked at her mother, "Do you think they are nice?"

Lily considered. "Probably not. Let's catch our bus home. Someday you will be waiting for a bus to take you home," she said.

They crossed the street and walked another block. They waited in a glass bus shelter. "Here we wait for bus fifty two," Lily told Gina.

Gina looked out the windows on the way home. First they passed tall buildings, department stores, and apartment buildings. Then the bus took them on into her neighborhood, close to downtown. A place where workers, children, and the elderly lived, not too comfortably.

Gina and Lily walked the few blocks from the bus stop. They passed small houses surrounded by scraggly hedges and seldom mowed lawns. Some neighbors grew flowers to brighten up the yards. The lilacs were in full bloom. Gina sneezed.

"Bless you! Your dad is taking you to see the horse races tomorrow. Unless he forgets. Or doesn't come home. Or sleeps too late," Lily told Gina. She unlocked the door to their tiny grey house.

She stepped in after her mother. Pepe, Gina's black poodle, leapt into her arms. "Is dad playing with his band tonight? If he does, we'll never go see the horses. He'll sleep too late."

Lily picked up a note from the kitchen table. She read to Gina, "I'm at the Fine Line tonight. It's a respectable jazz club. It doesn't stay open after hours. I might be home before three after loading out. Don't wait up for me. Ted."

Gina sighed. She put Pepe down to eat his dinner. "I guess I'll be ready to go in case. I really want to see the horses, mom!"

"I know. I'll be at the studio in the morning. I

won't be here to wake him. I'll set an alarm for him before I leave. I'll put the volume way up," Lily said.

"Okay. Mom, I don't have to take ballet downtown yet, do I? I like having class here at home with you."

"No. Not yet. But soon you will know everything that I can teach you. Then you will have to go to Madame," Lily said.

After dinner Gina helped Lily set up the living room for ballet class. Gina had told her mother that she was too shy to learn ballet with the girls at Lily's studio. Lily taught her at home. They slid the furniture to one end of the room. A large mirror hung on one wall. Gina put together a collapsable barre against the wall opposite the mirror. Lily took a record player and records out of the front closet.

Lily looked around, "It's good. I suppose we could have all of this in the basement. We could leave it in place all the time. But, I don't like dancing in a basement."

"Besides, there are monsters in the laundry room," Gina reminded her.

"That, too!" Lily laughed. "Let's begin. Left hand on the barre, two demi plies, one grand, port des bras forward and back, from first, second, and third position." She set the needle on their favorite ballet record. The record spun and the music started. They began.

They completed the exercise. Gina asked, "Will I ever be able to do fourth and fifth position?"

"Of course you will. Not yet. Your hips are not ready for those positions. It would put too much stress on your body," Lily answered.

Gina practiced fourth and fifth when Lily wasn't around. She knew her mother was right. She didn't look very graceful doing them. They finished the barre part of the class. They practiced pirouettes. Then they performed slow, balancing exercises in the middle of the living room. They finished the lesson with jumps and leaps.

Gina curtsied to Lily, as Lily taught her to do. That way, when Gina had another ballet teacher, she would know to curtsey at the end of class.

Lily asked, "Does it feel weird to curtsy to me at the end of class?"

Gina considered, "No, I guess not. I don't think of you as my mom when you are teaching me ballet. I think of you as, I don't know, Madame Pavlova. You know, that famous ballerina, Anna Pavlova?"

Lily laughed. "Yes, but she was far greater than

I will ever be. Thank you for the compliment. I will call you Ballerina Clara."

"Clara! From the *Nutcracker Fantasy*? Perfect!" Gina smiled.

Gina was in bed for the night. She thought about dancing ballet so well that Lily could no longer teach her. The idea sounded beautiful. Facing cars and buses and strangers downtown didn't. "It's my future. I will do it someday," she thought.

She heard Pepe's even breathing next to her. Soon she fell asleep. Gina dreamed about dancing in her first pair of pointe shoes.

2

A gentle breeze and the smell of roses wafted through the air. Gina and her dad waited for the horses to enter the Parade Circle. Gina flicked her ponytail over her shoulder. She stretched as tall as she could. She looked over the fence. Gina had begged her father for a year to take her to see the horses. On this brilliant, sunny May day he had decided to take her with him. Canterbury Downs racetrack was the highlight of Ted's week.

She excitedly looked as the thoroughbreds were led past her out of the paddock. Each one was as sleek and muscled as the last. Gina couldn't choose a favorite.

Her dad could, though. "*Hoist Her Flag* with Mike Smith riding. He can't be beat," he said. He drew a circle on his racing form. "Gina, stay here. I'll be right back. Don't go anywhere," he said. Ted bounded off to the betting windows.

The last of the horses were led to the boxes. People ran to place bets. Gina was alone. She heard a trumpet. A voice over loudspeakers announced the race. She heard, "And they're off!" She waited. Another race came and went. And then a third.

An older woman came to look at the horses for the fourth race. She looked down at Gina in her shorts and tee shirt. Her tee shirt had a horse and it's foal printed on it. She was sitting on the ground. "Are you alone?" the woman asked Gina.

"No, my dad's here. He told me to wait here for him."

"I think I know where he is. Come with me. It's okay. We are going to the betting window to find him. If he's not there, to the bar."

Gina nodded and scrambled to her feet. He was not at the betting window. They went to the bar. Gina pointed to a tall, very thin young man. He had dark hair and wore a baseball cap. "That's him," Gina said.

"Is she yours?" the woman asked Ted. His beer sloshed out of his cup. Ted finally answered. "Oh, yeah. Gina. Where have you been?"

"You told her to wait for you. You didn't come back to get her. She's been sitting outside for an hour," the woman said. She glared at Ted.

"Oh, yeah," he grinned sheepishly. "I forgot. I told her to wait for me. Thanks for reuniting us."

"Anything could have happened to her, you know. All alone for an hour," the woman muttered, walking away.

"I'm sorry, Gina," her dad said, looking down.

Gina looked up at him out of solemn green eyes. "You always are, dad," she stated.

"Let's go down to the track and watch the last races. I won't leave you."

Gina followed him down through the stands. They made their way to the fence encircling the dusty track. She saw *California Invader, Lost Kitty, Turbo Launch, Charging Through, Fork In The Road, Staff Riot,* and *John Bullit.*

The jockeys rode the horses into the boxes. The horses snorted and neighed. The trumpet sounded. The race was announced. The box doors flew open. Gina watched from only a few feet away. The thoroughbreds thundered past.

She breathed and exclaimed, "They are so beautiful! All of them. I don't care who wins!"

Her dad smiled down at her. He looked back to the race. He pointed out the finish line directly in front of them. Gina tracked the horses and riders as they came around. They approached the finish line. *Fork In The Road* won.

Many people cheered. Winners jogged off to collect their winnings. Other people swore. They ripped up their claim tickets and threw them to the ground.

They watched two more races. Gina found each horse beautiful and exhilarating. "They are like ballerinas!" she remarked.

"I suppose they are like dancers. Stretching, reaching, leaning into the wind," her father agreed.

Late in the afternoon the final race finished. Families gathered up their children. Everyone walked slowly through the hot sun to the huge parking lot. Gina headed out with her dad to find their car. Ted could not remember where he had parked. They wandered for quite a while.

Gina looked with him. She was tired, sunburnt, and hungry. "Dad, I want to go home."

"I know that!" he snapped. "I can't find the car."

Gina noticed the older woman again. She was the one who had helped Gina find Ted. "Is she following us?" Gina asked Ted.

"Probably. She wants to make sure I'm not going to ruin your life. Where is that stupid car?"

"Aren't you?" Gina sighed.

The woman called to them, "You're not going to drive your daughter home like that. Are you? You can't even find your car."

Ted stood slightly swaying. The parking lot was nearly empty. The sun beat down. He sighed, defeated. "She's right. I can't drive. Too much beer."

They trudged back to the track restaurant. He called Lily. Gina could hear her mother answer. She was not happy. "I have to get someone to teach my ballet class. And I have to pay them, you know. I'll get a taxi out there and drive you home." Gina heard her slam the receiver.

Gina trudged with her dad to the dusty parking lot again. The lot was nearly empty. Gina spotted the car. "There it is," she told Ted.

Lily soon arrived. They silently got into the car. Lily was listening to the radio. Prince's *Sign O the Times* was playing. It was one of Lily's favorite songs. It was about the young gangs of Minneapolis. Lily switched the station. She knew Ted wouldn't like it. The next station played Steve Winwood's *The Finer Things*. She left it. Ted liked that one.

Gina broke the silence. "When was Canterbury Downs built?" she asked.

"Let's see. What year is it? 1989. I think it's been open for a few years," Ted answered.

"How could you forget? You have gone every season," Lily remarked testily.

Gina changed the subject. "And what's the big deal about Mike Smith? I heard everyone talking about him," Gina asked.

Ted brightened up. "Mike Smith grew up on his grandparents' horse farm. He started riding horses when he was eight. He rode in races when he was only eleven. He dropped out of high school to be a jockey."

"No high school?" Gina was surprised.

Lily spoke from the driver's seat, "Don't get any ideas. You are tiny, but will grow!"

Gina smiled a little. "I thought being a jockey might be a good way to get out of school."

Ted asked, "I thought you liked school?"

"It's okay. I get bored sometimes."

Lily pulled into the tiny garage of their little house. She sighed and took the key out of the ignition. "Pepe will be starving."

Gina climbed out. She took the keys from her mother, and raced to the door. Her black poodle was there to greet her. He jumped all over her. Gina quickly gave him food and petted him. Gina looked up. She faintly heard her mother's sharp words. She heard the front door close. She heard the sound of a car pulling away.

Lily appeared in the doorway to the kitchen. "How's Pepe? I'm going to make dinner, okay?" she asked.

She hung the car keys on a hook on the wall. "Your dad went out with a friend. He picked him up. It's you and me tonight. Should we have a ballet lesson after dinner?"

Gina hugged Pepe. She got up to help Lily with dinner. "That sounds great, mom. *Growing Pains* and *Family Ties* are on tonight, too. For after ballet."

"Perfect," Lily said. She kissed the top of Gina's head.

After the ballet lesson they skipped regular television. They watched *The Red Shoes* instead. Gina had never seen it before. She loved the story of the young ballet dancer who wore the red shoes. She was torn between the man she loved and being a prima ballerina.

"Mom, I would pick being a ballerina, hands down, no question."

Lily laughed, "I guess I would, too. As long as I could have you as part of the deal."

They each went to their bedrooms. They called

"Good Night" to each other when they were settled.

Gina tossed and turned. She pounded her pillow in her attic bedroom. Pepe was sound asleep next to her. She had won the little black poodle in a raffle at church. Gina let her grandmother name him Pepe Le Moko.

Pepe was the French thief character in her grandmother's favorite movie. In the movie, the elegant Pepe was homesick for his beloved Paris. Both her grandmother and Lily wanted to see Paris before they died. Gina hugged Pepe. Falling asleep she thought, "Someday I will go to Paris with mom."

She awakened after a few hours. She saw police lights flashing outside her window. She heard no sirens. The police were kind enough not to sound the sirens when they brought her father home. "They must have found him wandering around downtown again. Too drunk to drive or find a taxi," Gina thought. She tried to fall back asleep.

Sometimes Gina lived in the light, but often in shadows. She could disappear when she wanted to. No one could find her. She curled into herself and turned over one last time. She snuggled Pepe, and finally fell asleep.

3

The next morning Ted slept very late. Lily got Gina up for school as usual in the morning. Neither of them spoke about the police being there the night before. Gina tried hard not to look at her mother's black eye. Her father did not appear at breakfast.

Lily kissed her good-bye. Gina started walking the six short blocks to school. She wore shorts under her Black Watch plaid uniform jumper. That way she could run at recess. The shorts covered her if her dress flew up.

After walking a block she saw her pals approaching. Blonde haired, blue eyed Sharie and black haired, green-eyed freckled Phil joined her.

"Hi, you guys. Do we have an English test today?" Gina asked casually.

"Yes! Gina, can I sit by you and copy your answers?" laughed Sharie.

"You know we have assigned seats," Gina answered.

"Besides, last week I asked Sister Dympna if I could sit next to Gina for the same reason. She's on to us now," Phil added.

"You said her name wrong again, Phil," Sharie told him.

"It's spelled so weird. How do you say Dympna again?" he asked.

"Think of it this way. Pretend it's spelled DIP-NA." Gina spelled DIPNA out loud.

"Okay, that works. Sister DIPNA," Phil practiced.

Sharie took a last minute peek in her notebook. "Gina, you are a whole year younger than me and Phil, but you're so smart! Is that why you started kindergarten when you were four years old?"

"I guess so. My mom said I was bored at home. She said I should just go ahead and start school."

Phil slapped his forehead. "I just remembered. Parent and teacher conferences are tonight! We better make sure we are on time. We better be good all day!"

Gina's heart sank. She felt a lump in her throat. Lily would have to go to the conferences with a black eye. If she stayed home she would get calls from school asking why she had not attended.

"Hey, did you see those cop car lights flashing last night? I wonder why there wasn't a siren?" Phil asked.

Sharie quickly answered, "I didn't see anything, Phil. You were dreaming. You watch those cop crime shows before bed. Gina, did you see anything?"

"Uh, no, I didn't either." She squeezed Sharie's hand briefly behind Phil's back. Sharie's other hand poked Phil.

"What the? Oh, I remember. I watched *Batman* reruns before I went to bed. But, yeah, I was probably dreaming."

Gina changed the subject. "Have you ever wondered why we go to school dressed like Scottish warriors?"

"What?!" Sharie and Phil asked together.

"The plaid of our uniforms. It's Black Watch plaid. It's from the Black Watch Regiment of Scotland. My mom told me."

"It's just you two. I wear navy pants and a light blue shirt," Phil reminded them.

"That's right. So, it's just us girls! That's even cooler!" Sharie said. She swung Gina's hand.

"I thought you'd think so," Gina smiled.

"I wonder what it's like for nuns to wear long black dresses, a veil, and that white collar all day?" Sharie mused.

"I don't know. The priests and altar boys wear dresses. It doesn't seem weird when I'm altar boy," Phil said.

"Do you ever snitch wine?" Sharie pried.

Phil raised an eyebrow. "It's expected. Any altar boy worth his salt sneaks sacrificial wine."

"I always wonder if the nuns have hair under their hats. Are they all bald?" Gina smiled.

The three climbed the cement stairs to the heavy wooden double door. Phil and Sharie both pulled and they entered Our Lady of Victory Elementary School. The sixth graders had classrooms on second floor.

They climbed the stairs. They walked on the landing with the gigantic window. The sculpture of Our Lady of Victory stood there. Our Lady wore a flowing dress. She had her arm around the Infant King. He stood on a globe of the world.

Gina loved the sculpture. She touched Mary's toe as she went past. She did this each morning. It was her good luck charm for the day. She hung up a navy blue jacket in the cloakroom.

She joined her classmates. They were lining up to go to mass. They filed into the church. It was attached to the school. The eight graders sat in the front rows, behind them was the seventh grade and so on. First graders sat in the back.

Gina thought, "It doesn't make sense that the littlest students sit in the back rows. They can't see anything over everyone else." She sat down with the rest of the sixth graders in the middle rows of the church.

There was a surprise at mass this morning. Gina wasn't quite aware of it at first. Phil poked her in the side. "Look, Sister Aquinas is going up to the altar," he whispered.

"What? It's not time for Communion," Gina whispered back.

"I know. What's she doing?" he whispered, wondering.

The church froze. The students watched. Sister Aquinas climbed the few marble stairs. She stopped. Sister stood on the altar in front of the very surprised Father Ambrose. There were no coughs, no shuffling of feet on the floor, no rustling of pages. Only silence a knife could cut through.

Sister Aquinas bowed her head. She was trembling. "Father, the children are missing too many classes. Mass is longer this year. I am afraid they will not pass their exams." She spoke barely above a whisper.

Gina felt herself stand up. The nun closest to her whispered, "Gina, sit down!"

Gina stared at Sister Aquinas. She thought, "Sister cares so much about us. She is standing up to Father for us." Gina found herself unable to speak. She began to clap her hands. She applauded Sister Aquinas. Phil pulled at her to sit down, but she kept on.

Sister Imelda came over to Gina. Grabbing Gina's arm, she led her out. Gina continued to clap on the way. Gina could feel the back of sister's heavy ring pressing into her arm. Gina heard Father speak to Sister Aquinas.

Father Ambrose was enraged. He said, "Leave this church. Go."

Gina turned her head. She saw Sister Aquinas softly weeping. She backed down the altar stairs. Sister crossed herself and walked out. Father continued mass. People started breathing again.

Once in the hallway, Sister Imelda said, "Gina, sit down here outside Sister Margaret Mary's office. I don't know why you clapped in church just now. Sister will call you when she is ready."

"Sister Aquinas was trying to help us!" Gina said. Sister Imelda looked at Gina questioningly. Sister entered the office. After a moment she opened the door again and shut it. Sister Imelda did not look at Gina. She walked off down the hall.

Soon Gina heard, "Gina, come in." Gina had never been sent to the principal's office before. Her hand shook as she turned the handle on the door.

"Gina, please sit down," Sister Margaret Mary directed her.

Gina sat on the edge of a chair. She could not look at Sister Margaret Mary. Sister stood before her. She crossed her arms in front of her bodice. Her hands were hidden in her sleeves. "Gina, I have called your mother. I want you to spend the rest of the day at home. Sharon and Phillip will bring homework to you. Your mother is coming to get you. Please wait for her in the hall."

"Yes, Sister. Is that all?"

"You and I will talk again when your mother arrives."

Gina rose. She opened the door and shut it quietly behind her.

Lily arrived breathless. She found Gina on a bench. Sitting down beside her she asked, "What happened? I want to hear it from you first."

Gina told her the whole story. Lily could not help but smile. "You did? Wow. Gina, before we go in, I want you to know that you did nothing wrong. I understand why Father and Sister Mary Margaret don't see it that way. Let's go in."

Gina sat down with Lily and Sister. Father Ambrose arrived. He poked his head in the door. He said, "Sister Margaret Mary. I trust you to handle this as you see fit." He nodded at Lily and Gina and left.

Gina exhaled. She thought, "That must mean something. He didn't stay. Maybe they aren't going to expel me after all."

Lily began. "Sister, thank you for meeting with Gina and me. She told me what happened in church today. I believe that Gina did not understand how serious this is. I remember when I was a girl. I was six years old at Sunday mass with my parents at the Cathedral. I went to the Cathedral School."

The Cathedral School was a very excellent school. Sister looked impressed that Lily had been a student there. Sister looked out the window. She said, "I see."

Lily continued. "My parents had explained to me how Pope John Paul wanted to make the church modern. He wanted all people to understand the mass better. The priest at the Cathedral wanted to keep the old ways. To protest the pope he said mass in Latin."

Sister nodded. "Many traditional Catholics rejected the Pope's new ways."

Lily continued, "Some people in church stood up. They walked up to the altar. They yelled at the priest to say mass in English. The priest argued loudly with the people. He continued on in Latin."

Sister looked up. "Yes. That priest is no longer at the Cathedral."

"I told Gina this story. I also have taken her to weddings and guitar masses. People applauded in church. The church has changed. And perhaps it will more. Please allow Gina to remain in school. She can learn from this experience. Perhaps there are other ways she can support Sister Aquinas."

"I won't clap in church again!" Gina promised.

"Yes. I understand. Gina please come to my office right away in the morning. I will decide how you can apologize to Father Ambrose and Sister Aquinas. That's all for now."

The two said "Good Bye" and left.

"Do you think I got off easy, mom?"

"Maybe. Who cares? Let's run when we get outside. It was a tough meeting. Now it's over! You have the rest of the day off!"

Children and staff looking out the window saw Gina and her mother. They whooped and laughed as they ran home.

4

The following morning Gina walked silently with Sharie and Phil. Sharie swung her arms. She skipped as though nothing had happened to Gina the day before. They entered school and climbed the stairs.

Phil sighed deeply. He looked worried. "I'm still shocked about yesterday in church. What do you think they will do to Sister Aquinas?"

Before anyone could answer, a nun came around the corner. She shushed them. Gina touched Mary's toe. Sharie whispered, "Gina, what did they do to you?"

"I'll tell you after class."

Sister Dympna waved them into spelling class.

"Hurry, children. Quickly. Sit down and get to work."

The three headed into class. They took their seats. Sister did not say a word about the incident from mass. Students stared at Gina with interest. But, no one said anything.

Gina opened her notebook. She began work on the day's assignment. Soon she heard Sister say, "Gina, come up to the board."

"I hate this part," Gina thought. Silently she wondered, "Can't I be left alone to do my work?"

Sister Dympna had written a list of ten very complicated words. Gina rose and approached the board. She was allowed ten seconds to look at the words. She read the list. It included words such as pseudonym, mischievous, and lieutenant. Sister erased it completely.

Taking a piece of chalk. Gina wrote the words from memory. "This is fun," she thought.

She scribbled away, writing her answers. She replaced the chalk in the tray and turned to go to her seat. Gina saw that many of the students were open-mouthed in awe.

She heard whispers, "How did she do that?"

On the way to their next class, Phil and Sharie asked Gina, "How did you remember and spell all of the words perfectly? Those words were crazy!"

Gina looked bewildered. "I don't know. The answers just come to me. I write them down."

"It's amazing. I wish I was that smart," Sharie said.

Phil echoed, "Yeah, me, too."

Gina finally said, "I know how to memorize and spell long words. I don't get what happened in mass with Sister Aquinas. Why is everyone so shocked? She was polite when she talked to Father Ambrose. And what she said was true. We are missing more classes because mass is longer now. What's wrong with that?"

Sharie replied, "Sister is a woman who complained to a man. She complained in front of everyone in church."

"On the altar! Some people say she'll burn in hell," Phil added.

"See, you are smarter than me. I didn't get that at all," Gina said. "I just thought Sister was looking out for us kids. I have to write apology letters to Father Ambrose and Sister Aquinas."

"That's all? What did they say in the meeting?" Sharie asked.

"My mom said some complicated stuff about the church changing. It must have worked. They told me all I have to do is write letters."

They entered Confirmation class. They sat in a row together.

"I wonder what scary treat Sister Imelda will have for us today?" Sharie whispered.

"You know, I don't get this Confirmation stuff," Phil admitted. "A bishop is going to put oil on our foreheads and then a spirit enters us?"

"I don't get it either, but with Confirmation you get to speak in tongues. You know, in other languages," Gina whispered.

"Like that's going to happen. I know Gaelic. I don't think you suddenly will speak Gaelic because a bishop puts oil on your forehead," Phil scoffed.

"It might! Do we get to pick what language, or is it all of them?" Sharie asked. Other students began entering.

"Anyway, it's not as weird as what happens on Holy Thursday," Gina whispered.

Sharie and Phil both asked, "What?"

"I read it at the back of the book. I never knew what the priests were doing," Gina replied. Gina pointed in her book.

She read quietly, "It's called *Blessing of the Oil of Catechumens.* The blessing is for exorcisms. We get power to drive away the devil. On Holy Thursday the priest blesses the oil. He prays the Rite of Exorcism over all of us."

"Why?" Phil and Sharie asked together.

"In case we got possessed!" Gina declared.

Sharie and Phil's mouths dropped to the floor. They continued whispering to each other.

Sister Imelda rapped her ring on the desk loudly. "I have a surprise for all of you. You will choose the name of a saint as your own for Confirmation. Today we are going to read about saints' lives!"

Gina knew from past classes that this was good. The life of Saint Joan of Arc was thrilling. Joan fought with men. She suffered a fiery death.

Gina looked through the book of saints' lives. She picked Saint Genevieve. She and Lily liked the musical *Camelot*. Lily often listened to the soundtrack. The song *The Simple Joys of Maidenhood* was about St. Genevieve.

Gina settled in at her desk. She read silently about St. Genevieve. "She was born over five hundred years ago around the year 420. She died around 510."

She read with a shiver. "Genevieve is shown in paintings with the devil. The devil blew out her candle when she prayed at night."

Gina looked at an illustration of Genevieve. An

angel looked over one of her shoulders. A demon looked over the other shoulder.

She read, "Genevieve's mother went blind. It happened after she stopped Genevieve from going to church."

"Why would her mom keep her out of church?" Gina wondered.

She turned the page. "Genevieve brought back her mother's sight with water from their well. When Genevieve walked to school, a bridge appeared over a ditch filled with water. The bridge disappeared after she crossed it. Genevieve also had the power to change the weather."

"Cool!" Gina said aloud. This drew a stern glance from Sister.

Gina skipped down the page. "Genevieve could read people's thoughts. This angered many men in Paris."

She thought with a frown, "Bet they weren't thinking about their wives!"

Gina paused. She looked at Sister. She tried to read Sister Imelda's thoughts. "All I can get is that she wishes she didn't have to wear that scratchy thing on her head. It's hot in this warm weather," she thought silently.

Gina returned to St. Genevieve. "The Huns were going to attack Paris. Genevieve told the women of Paris to fast and pray to fight the Huns. The Huns left Paris."

Gina looked out the window. "I don't know what a Hun is, but they sound dangerous. Hmm..., so it was the women who saved the city."

Gina smiled. She read, "Genevieve also performed exorcisms."

"Aha! Here's the good stuff." She frowned. "I thought only men did exorcisms. Like in *The Exorcist*. Here's a woman doing it!" she marveled to herself.

Gina read further, "A woman stole Genevieve's shoes. The woman was struck blind. Someone led her back to Genevieve. The shoe thief asked for forgiveness. Genevieve cured her blindness.

Gina looked up and thought, "Wow, bad stuff happens to people who cross Genevieve."

Sister called to the class, "We will now work on memorizing prayers."

Gina rose when it was her turn. She walked to an alcove on the side of the classroom. She recited her prayers to Sister Imelda. Gina's memory was perfect. She received a warm smile from Sister.

A boy named Tim went next. Gina looked up briefly. He walked past her desk. Tim whispered to Gina, "Don't be late for patrol duty." He grinned and continued to the alcove.

She felt a little thrill. Sharie noticed Gina smiling. Sharie whispered, "Gina has a crush!"

Gina whispered back, "No, I don't! And I'm never late for patrol duty. He's the one who's late. And he skips out early!"

Like Gina, Tim received a warm smile from Sister. Sharie whispered. "Well, you'd be perfect for each other. The two smartest kids in sixth grade."

Phil was next. Gina and Sharie each gave him comforting looks. They hoped the looks said, "You'll get them right this time."

They suffered watching Phil. He haltingly recited. He stole looks at his sweating palm. He had written cheat notes there.

Gina thought, "It's stupid and unfair to make kids memorize stuff. God doesn't care if you read it from a piece of paper or know it by heart! It's easy for me. All the kids are good at kickball. I'm horrible at it. But, I don't get a lower grade because I'm awful at it."

Phil turned to return to his seat. He winked at Gina and Sharie. He whispered to them, "The cheats in my hand worked!" The girls sighed and smiled.

A lecture followed. Sometimes Sister Imelda veered way off topic. Her talks confused everyone.

Gina liked them because the stories were interesting. Today Sister told a story. It was about Jesus fitting himself into a holy wafer.

Sister waved her arm in a black sleeve enthusiastically. Her white handkerchief dropped out of it. Sister dramatically related, "I taught a four year-old girl. She asked, 'How can Jesus make himself small enough to fit into a holy wafer?'"

She looked around the room expecting to see shocked faces. Instead she saw a sea of confused faces. Sister boasted, "I immediately allowed her to take her First Communion. Even at four, she understood the miracle of Jesus."

Gina felt uncomfortable and stupid. On the way out of class she asked Sharie and Phil, "If I'm so smart, why didn't I think of that when I was four?"

"You wouldn't have given it that much space in your brain," Phil answered.

Sharie added, "Plus, what does that little girl have to do with our Confirmation?"

"We're probably the only school left in the world that still has nuns. We're lucky we like most of them," Gina whispered.

The final class of the day was choir with Sister Eustachia. "See you guys. I'm in band," Phil said.

"Phil, you should switch to choir," Sharie suggested.

"Not with what my parents paid for this clarinet. Besides, I can barely say DIPNA. I would never be able to say Eustachia."

Gina and Sharie said together, "You-stay-she-uh."

"No way. Later!" Phil smiled. He headed down the hall.

Gina loved to sing. She hated choir class. Sister Eustachia taught the class. She was terrifying. In Sister's mind she had given up a career as an opera singer to be a nun. Many times Sister Eustachia sang solos during Sunday mass. Lily always winced during those solos. Once she turned to Gina and whispered, "Did you hear that clinker?"

Gina sat in the last row of the class. Sister sang to demonstrate how she wanted a certain phrase to be sung. Gina heard a clinker and winced. Two or three students happened to be looking in Gina's direction. They saw the look on Gina's face and laughed.

Sister saw Gina make the sour face. She reprimanded Gina. "Wipe that ugly look off of your face."

The room was very silent. Gina could hear a fly buzzing near one of the windows. Gina mumbled, "I'm sorry, Sister. I winced because I got a splinter from my desk." She hated herself for apologizing. She hated herself even more for lying.

Sharie smiled behind her music book.

Sister sniffed. She went on with class. Gina and Sharie rushed out as soon as the bell rang. She said to Sharie, "On top of clapping in church, this is awful."

"But, you were right! She hit a bad note!" Sharie left her at the cloakroom.

Gina made her way to the basement of the school. There she put on her safety vest. She took out her flag for after school patrol duty. She went to her corner. Her job was to help younger students cross the streets. Except there never were any cars. It was a pretty quiet neighborhood at three in the afternoon. She put the flag out when they crossed anyway.

Soon most of the children had crossed. Gina was alone with her thoughts. She wondered, "Why hasn't Tim come by to check on everything? I would have done a better job as patrol captain."

She wound and unwound her orange flag around it's pole.

She wondered, "Why wasn't I picked to be captain? It always goes to the smartest boy or girl in the class. That's me and Tim. I guess I'll never know how he edged me out."

She both hoped and dreaded that he would come by on his rounds. "I might as well admit it. I have a secret crush on Tim," she sighed.

The trees were budding and blooming. Her allergies were in full force. Sometimes she felt she would faint away from the smell of flowers. Gina watched the swaying of the tree branches in the breeze. She loved the sound of wind blowing through the leaves. The cottonwoods made the most beautiful sound. White cottony balls floated down and around her. There were so many on the ground it looked snow.

Gina sneezed violently. "How can I love trees so much, when they make me so miserable?" she thought. She got out a tissue.

Tim didn't come by that day. She wound her flag around its pole a final time. She made her way back to the school. Tim bumped into her on his way out. "Gina, I'm leaving a little early. I have a baseball game. Please don't tell anyone," he said breathlessly. He winked.

Gina looked at his auburn hair shining in the sun and nodded. She whispered, "I won't tell."

On her way home she thought, "I won't tell. That's all I could think of to say? Not a cute, flirty comeback? I'm not a flirt, though. He must think I'm an idiot."

Gina arrived home. Lily was dabbing make-up under her eye. She wore a dress, sweater, and sandals. Gina looked at her sadly. "Mom, you could say you are sick. You could reschedule your parent teacher conference tonight. Or, make dad go alone."

"Gina, I am going. Your father will not be here for a week or so. He is staying with a friend. I don't want him here right now. I don't care if your teachers know that he hit me. They should be ashamed of him, not of me. And I'm taking steps. I can't explain right now."

Gina felt nauseous, but somehow better. She stayed home alone with Pepe. Her mother went to the conference at school. Lily returned after an hour or so. She found Gina reading in her room. Lily immediately went to hug Gina.

Lily said, holding her tightly, "Gina, thank you for being a wonderful daughter! Everyone loves you at school. I am so proud of you and happy for you."

"Even Sister Eustachia?" Gina asked incredulously.

"Why, yes. Her, too. She said you have a lovely singing voice. You are always right on pitch."

Gina heard Lily starting to cry. Gina cried, too. "Mom, I am so relieved you are home. And that dad is not here. Am I mean? I don't want him here."

Lily sniffled, "No, you are a strong and beautiful girl. You know who loves you."

"Aren't you supposed to love your parents no matter what?" Gina asked.

"Not in this case, Gina. It is okay to not love him." Lily brushed Gina's hair out of her eyes.

Gina pulled her knees up. She wrapped her arms around them. "One of the nuns said something in school today. She said 'the meek shall inherit the earth.' I don't think that's true."

Lily laughed, "Neither do I. It sounds like the meek get stuck being on earth. Everyone else gets to go to heaven."

Gina smiled, too. "That's what I thought! I don't think I want to be meek."

"You already are stronger than you know, Gina," Lily reminded her.

"I feel bad for Sister Aquinas. I want to be like her," Gina said.

"Did you start the letters to her and Father Ambrose?" Lily asked.

"Sort of," Gina answered. She took out a notebook. She read aloud.

. . .

Dear Father Ambrose,

This is Gina. I am being punished for helping Sister Aquinas in church. Sister Margaret Mary told my mom I have to write this letter.

I know I clapped during mass. But mass had already been interrupted. You and Sister Aquinas were talking about school. I guess I don't really understand what I am apologizing for. Maybe I should apologize to God? But, God wants us to do well in school. Doesn't he? Shouldn't Sister Aquinas and you apologize to each other? Or, maybe to the students and teachers for interrupting mass?

I don't get this at all. I don't think I did anything wrong. We clap in church when we have guitar masses and when people get married. Anyway, I don't think it will help me to pray on it, like Sister Margaret Mary suggested. I never get any answers that way. I seem to come up with better ideas myself. All I want to do is help Sister Aquinas. And she was right. Mass is longer than it used to be. Could you maybe talk faster?

Sincerely,

Gina Shostek

P.S. My mom liked the artwork in Sister Margaret Mary's office, especially the painting of St. John the Baptist.

.   .   .

Gina said to Lily, "Sister Aquinas was right! And he was wrong. He could have asked Sister to talk about it with him later. I bet Sister did try to talk to Father Ambrose about it and he wouldn't!"

"Gina, I have to admit this is all right and true. Do you mind if I help you with it a little tomorrow? Don't give it to anyone yet. Okay?"

"Sure, mom," Gina said, handing Lily the notebook.

"What about Sister Aquinas?" Lily asked.

"I found a poem I think she will like. I think it's about loving and being human." Gina read aloud.

The Divine Image

Mercy has a human heart,
Pity a human face,
And Love, a human form divine,
And Peace, a human dress.

—William Blake

"I cut out the last stanza. It didn't make any sense. I thought I would draw flowers around it. I can give it to her, "Gina said.

"Gina, it's a lovely poem. Let's work on this one tomorrow, too."

"Mom, I'm so tired."

Lily said, "Me, too. Go to sleep."

She kissed Gina's forehead. She put the worn copy of Noel Streatfeild's *Ballet Shoes* on the nightstand. Lily fondly remembered the story of the little girl, Posy. The little girl was abandoned by her parents. Posy went on to become a great ballerina.

As she was falling asleep, Gina heard her mother's Hildegard von Bingen record. Four women sang lilting, exquisite melodies. Gina knew they were Lily's favorite things to listen to when something in her world wasn't right. Gina fell asleep worrying, "Things aren't quite right. There must be some way I can help mom."

5

The next day at lunch, Lisa approached Gina. She was in Gina's class. Lisa was tall and slender with dark brown eyes. She was very kind and gentle. Linda was her equally tall, slender and kind older sister. Linda peeked over Lisa's shoulder. Gina wondered if Lisa and Linda's mother had seen Lily's black eye at conferences the night before.

"Hi, Gina!" they said softly. They sat down at Gina's table. Gina smiled at them in the middle of a bite of sandwich.

"Can you come over to our house tonight for a sleepover?" Lisa asked.

Linda added, "Just the three of us, not a lot of kids."

Gina swallowed. "I will ask my mom."

Lisa and Linda smiled. "Great. We will call you after school. Our dad will come and pick you up tonight. If it's okay."

One of the nuns announced that lunch was over. Everyone went to their classes.

Gina smiled. She thought about the sleepover in English class. Near the end of English class with Sharie she remembered. Her next class was Gym. Her smile quickly faded. She thought, "Ugh, I'm awful at everything in Gym. At least Phil's there."

Sharie poked her when they started worksheets. "What's the difference between an adjective and an adverb?" she whispered.

"The tall man walked quickly. Tall describes the man. Tall is the adjective. Quickly describes how he walks. Quickly is the adverb," Gina whispered back.

"Oh, yeah. Thanks."

Gina walked slowly to Gym class. She changed clothes as slowly as she could. She was the very last person in line. The class marched out onto the field.

She whispered to Phil, "What torture do they have for us today?"

He whispered back, "Kickball."

Gina's heart sank. Phil couldn't help her with kickball. She was placed in the outfield. For a few minutes she was safe. Nothing came her way. The other team used up their outs. She had to come in. She might possibly be asked to kick.

She walked slowly to the line to wait to kick. Phil was in front of her. In front of him were two other very capable kickers. When it was Phil's turn he kicked the ball. It sailed out over the field. Three runs were scored off of Phil's incredible kick.

Gina was happy that the bases were not loaded. That would have been the worst. But now she had no hope. She had to kick. She felt nauseous.

"Well, here goes the rest of my life. No one will ever forget me striking out in kickball," she thought.

She kicked the first ball. It veered out of bounds. It was decided she should have another chance.

"Really, I'm okay. I don't need to kick again. Someone else can have a turn," she called out.

"Nah, it's okay, Gina. Your team pretty much already won," the pitcher called back.

He rolled the ball to her. Her foot struck the ball this time. It popped into the air. It was easily caught by the pitcher.

She heaved a sigh of relief. "I didn't even have

to run. And I didn't die from striking out. It's okay," she thought thankfully.

"I have never seen anyone strike out in kick-ball," Phil said in disbelief. He walked her back into school.

"It's all I could do. I didn't mean to make us have an out," Gina said. She couldn't look at him.

He laughed. "No one cares about that! I'll show you how to kick better some time if you want."

"Somehow, I think it would make it worse. But thanks," Gina replied. She thought, "Gym class was miserable. At least I will have fun tonight."

Gina hurried home after school. She asked, "Mom, can I sleep over at Lisa and Linda's house tonight?"

Lily handed Gina a chocolate chip cookie. She nibbled on one herself. "Yes! Their mother just called. They will pick you up at six tonight. Bring them some cookies. I just made them. I'm late to the studio. I have some new choreography. I can't wait to see how the girls look dancing it!"

Lily grabbed a large dance bag and keys. She kissed the top of Gina's head. She went out the door. "Lock the door!" she called back.

Gina securely locked the door. The house was quiet. Pepe leapt into her lap to keep her company. She ate another cookie. She did her homework at the kitchen table. She looked out into the yard at her favorite maple tree. She smiled at the tree. She thought about how often she could be found sitting on its lowest branch.

She put Pepe on the floor and gave him his dinner. She packed up some cookies. Pepe followed her into her room. She went through her clothes. Gina finally dressed in a pair of jeans, white Keds, and her favorite long-sleeved white tee shirt. "I probably look okay," she said to Pepe. She checked herself in the mirror.

She packed a pair of pink pajama pants and matching tee shirt with 'Sweet Dreams' embroidered on the front in an overnight bag. She gathered up her toothbrush, underwear, and a pale blue tee shirt for the next morning. She added those to the bag.

She let Pepe into the yard one more time. She let him back in. Lisa and Linda pulled up to her house with their dad. Gina hugged Pepe one more time. She locked the door carefully. She grabbed her bag and went out to their station wagon.

Lisa and Linda squealed. They jumped out of the car. They hugged Gina. They grabbed her bag. Lisa helped her into the backseat of the car.

Lisa and Linda's dad glanced back. He smiled at Gina. "I'm Bill, Gina. Nice to meet you. My wife said that your mom would be teaching ballet late this evening."

"Yes. It's nice to meet you, too. Thank you for having me over."

"Anytime. What are you girls doing tonight?" he asked.

"First *Pictionary,*" Linda answered.

"With *Pop Rocks,* of course," added Lisa. "A fight to the death with *Nerf Guns.* After that *Adventures in Babysitting.*"

Gina looked out the window. Bill drove out of her neighborhood. They went on into neighborhoods with bigger and newer homes. The car finally pulled up at Lisa and Linda's house. She got out of the car. She saw a lush green lawn and blooming flowerbeds. They lived in a white three story house with large windows. It was nothing like Gina's own tiny two bedroom house. Gina thought, "I can't imagine crime happening here, like by our house."

Lisa and Linda's mom greeted them at the door. The girls settled in a wood paneled den with popcorn, *Pop Rocks,* sodas, and a stack of VHS tapes. Gina laughed and joked along with the girls. She had more fun than she had had for a long time. Lisa and Linda's older brother popped his head in to greet them. Gina dissolved into blushes.

Lisa fired a pillow at him. "Ooh, Gina. It's Tony. He's a big time senior in high school. Look out!"

He laughed and said, "Hi, Gina, nice to meet you." Tony fired a pillow back at his sister. He ducked out of the room.

"Every girl in school is after him," Lisa nodded to Gina. "It's getting late. We can have *Nerf Gun* fights in the morning. Let's go upstairs. Let's have a seance!"

They went up to Linda's room. She was the oldest of the two sisters. Linda had a very sophisticated room.

"It's kinda retro," they said in unison.

They parted a beaded curtain and entered the room. Gina saw a black lava lamp and bean bag chairs. A wildly colored coverlet in neon orange, pink, and black covered her bed.

"I love this! Wow! And your parents let you have it?" Gina asked.

"They helped decorate the room!" the sisters laughed.

Gina sunk into one of the beanbag chairs. "Wow. It must be great to be you two. I wish I had a sister, like you have each other."

"You have us!"

Gina nodded. She felt foolish. "I shouldn't have

let them know that sometimes I'm lonely," she thought.

Linda got out the spirit board. Lisa lit candles. "Let's sit on the floor," Linda said. She set up the board. Lisa put the pointer on the board. The pointer would move when the girls placed their fingertips on it.

Lisa turned out the lights. She sat down with the other two. "Gina, you're our guest. You go first. What do you want to ask?"

They placed their fingertips on the device. Gina smiled slyly. "What is Matthew Broderick doing at this very moment?"

Lisa sighed, "Oh, I loved *Ferris Bueller*!" She elbowed Linda. "Don't move the pointer!"

"I'm not! Oh, look. It's spelling. HESHOOTSA-GUN," Linda read, "He shoots a gun!"

"Matthew Broderick? No way, he's too sweet," Gina argued.

Lisa grabbed a magazine near Linda's bed. "Matthew Broderick is in the movie *Biloxi Blues*. He plays a soldier. You read it in *Tiger Beat*." Lisa swatted Linda with the magazine.

Linda laughed and covered her face. "Okay, I admit it. I moved it. I promise, now I'll stop."

Lisa said, "Be serious. Everyone, fingertips back on the pointer. I'll ask the next one." She paused.

She asked dramatically, "Will Rob Lowe ever answer Linda's fan letter?"

Linda laughed. "Fine, you're getting me back."

"Rob Lowe? No! Way too pretty," said Gina.

"It doesn't matter. He's not going to write back anyway," Lisa said. The pointer moved to "No."

"Gina's turn." Linda nodded at Gina.

"Oh, okay. Does Lisa have a crush on Patrick Swayze?" The pointer immediately swerved to "Yes."

"I admit it. But only in secret. He's too good a dancer. He would make me look bad," said Lisa. She took tap and jazz lessons.

Linda directed, "Okay one more. That we all ask together."

They all sighed together. "George Michael."

"What should we ask?" Gina wondered.

"If he would go out on a date with all three of us," Lisa offered.

Linda said, "That's good, but I'm not sure he even likes girls."

"He might like both," Gina smiled. "I wouldn't care. All I would want him to do is sing to me."

The girls squealed when they looked at the board. The device pointed to "Yes."

Lisa brought two airbeds in from her room. "We can all sleep here in Linda's room," she said.

"Otherwise, it's not a slumber party," Linda added. She put sheets and blankets on the beds.

Gina changed into pajamas and brushed her teeth. The girls had their very own bathroom. It was stocked with bubble bath and blue and green striped towels. "Wow. Their parents and brother must have their own bathrooms, too," Gina thought.

She climbed onto an airbed. Lisa took the other. Linda slept in her own bed. They fell asleep listening to *Wake Me Up, Before You Go Go*. All three of them danced in their sleep.

The next morning was Saturday. The girls slept later than usual. Lisa and Linda's mom made pancakes. They sat on stools around a high counter in the kitchen. The window looked out into a large backyard. The sound of birds twittering came through the screen. The sun shone brightly over flowers beds bursting with spring flowers. Gina ate somewhat silently.

"Are weekends always like this?" Gina asked.

"Pretty much. What do you mean?" Linda responded.

"It's so beautiful here. I bet nice things happen every single day," Gina said. She poured syrup.

"Well, this weekend was extra fun, because you

are here. I'm really glad you came over," Lisa said. She poured orange juice for Gina.

Their father came in. "Girls, we're going to visit your grandmother in a while. Should we drive Gina home?"

"I guess so. Wait!" Linda ran off. She returned with two packs of *Pop Rocks* for Gina to take home.

Once in the car, the three girls joked and laughed. The father smiled occasionally at their silliness. At Gina's house the girls leapt out. They hugged her. "Bye, Gina. Thanks for coming over!"

Through the car window, Bill said, "Come see us again, Gina."

Gina waved. She made her way up the walk to the crumbling back steps. She opened the door and was greeted by Pepe and her mom.

Lily looked up from the newspaper, "How was it?"

Gina set down her bag. She let Pepe into her arms. "They're like my cousins, but not athletic. They have a really nice house and yard. They argue sometimes, but it's fun arguing. I think they have fun every day."

"Gina, I'm so sorry it isn't better for you here." Lily put her head down and cried.

"Mom! No! I didn't mean that. It's just different

than us. I love living with you. And we have ballet together and plays. None of my friends have that."

"Is it enough?" Lily sniffled.

Gina smiled at her. She hugged Lily with Pepe between them. "It's enough for me! I want to help you more, mom. Help you be happy."

Lily looked into Gina's eyes. "Your job is to be Gina. Come on. Let's dance!"

Lily and Gina had a ballet lesson in the living room. Gina worked extra hard.

6

After a few weeks Ted came home to live with Lily and Gina. He was only at the house a few days a week. He was only in the house during the day, when he mostly slept. At night and on weekends, he stayed with friends. He had plenty of gigs playing in jazz clubs.

It felt strange. Gina admitted to herself that it was better. Better than wondering whether or not her dad was going to hurt Lily. Bad things only seemed to happen at night.

The next morning Gina woke up. Pepe wasn't next to her. She called, but he didn't come. She looked out into the yard. She didn't see him. "Mom, where's Pepe?"

Lily looked out into the yard. "I don't see him. Go get dressed. I'll start looking."

Gina heard Lily come back into the house. "Gina, don't come outside," she said in a teary voice.

Gina came down stairs. Lily had filled a pitcher with cold water. She dumped it over Ted. He was sleeping on the sofa. "Get out there. Put Pepe in a box and dig a grave. I hate you."

Ted rubbed his swollen eyes. He asked, "Hey! What did you do that for?"

"Did you let Pepe outside last night?" Lily asked.

"He might have gone out when Randy dropped me off. I was pretty out of it," he grinned.

"Randy killed our dog with his car. Or someone did. You were so drunk you didn't see him run out. Get out there and take care of him. Do not try to talk to Gina. I will tell her."

Ted put on pants. He slowly went out and saw what he had done. He found a crate for Pepe and wrapped him in a blanket. He dug a hole and buried him under the maple tree.

Gina sobbed, watching from her room. She saw her mother set a suitcase out in the yard. Lily went back into the house. She locked the door. Ted saw the suitcase and picked it up. He got into the taxi Lily had called for him and left.

After a while Lily came into Gina's room. "Come with me." She led Gina to the car. They drove away.

"Where are we going?" Gina asked.

"Out in nature. Pepe is part of nature now. We will say 'Good-Bye' this way." Lily grabbed a couple of sketchbooks and pastels. "We are going to the zoo."

"The zoo?" Gina raised her eyebrows.

"The arboretum," Lily replied.

Lily parked and took Gina's hand. She led her to the arboretum. Many different kinds of flowers bloomed year round in the warm, humid environment. Once inside Lily showed Gina a certain flower. She took out her sketchbook and the pastels. She began to draw.

"This is an aster. It symbolizes patience and love." Lily selected a purple pastel and drew. "Pepe was patient with us when we first got him. He was learning how to be away from his mother. And he loved us," Lily said.

Gina opened the other sketchbook. She took a deep pink pastel. She read from a card posted next to the flower. "Astrantia represents strength, courage, and protection." She added, "Pepe protected us. He was never afraid."

Gina and Lily colored away. They drew scarlet bleeding hearts for undying love. Next were white and yellow daisies for innocence, hope, and happiness. Then blue hyacinth for playful joy.

"I'm drawing thistle for independence and nobility. He was a very princely poodle. Look, mom. This is for you." Gina pointed to the lilies. "Lilies are a wish for happiness."

Lily looked up from her drawing. She smiled. "Yes, a wish for happiness for me and you. I drew pink sweet peas. Sweet Peas send a message to say 'Good-Bye,' and 'Thank you for a lovely time.'"

They drew flowers from one end of the arboretum to the other. Gina carefully gathered up their drawings. They returned to the car. Lily put them in the backseat. Gina and Lily had one final good cry together.

"Okay, now the zoo." Lily swung Gina's hand. They walked back.

"First, the orangutans!" Lily said.

"And the monkeys!" Gina exclaimed.

The two arrived home in the early evening. The phone was ringing as they entered the house. Gina answered. "Oh, great! I'll be there after dinner."

Lily was making omelets for them. "Who was that?"

"Sharie. Phil's cat had kittens yesterday. They know what happened to Pepe. Can I go over there with Sharie? I think I'm done crying for a while."

"Sharie or Phil would not mind if you did cry. Of course you can go. It's dark out. Run quick to Sharie's house," Lily directed.

Gina ran the block to Sharie's house. Sharie took her hand. Together they ran to Phil's. The running outside helped Gina feel better. By the time they reached Phil's she was in an okay mood. Phil's mom hugged Gina. She served them ice cream cones. They played with the kittens.

Phil said, "I'm sorry about Pepe. Do you want a kitten?"

"Thanks, Phil. I don't think I'm ready yet." Four kittens climbed all over Gina and her ice cream cone.

Sharie held one tiny black kitten. "My mom said I can have one when they are ready to be away from their mom. Can I have this one? I'll call him 'Jinx.'"

"Yeah! We'll find out from the vet when they have shots if they are boys or girls. Jinx could work either way, I think," Phil said. He was petting a sleeping tabby.

"Definitely. He or she will be a good luck jinx, though. Everyone will want him to cross their path," Gina added. She smiled and said, "It feels good to smile. Thank you for the ice cream and the cheering up you two."

"We've got you, Gina! It's late. I have to go. Come on!" Sharie said. She took one last look at Jinx.

Phil gathered up the kittens. He placed them near their mother. "See you at Confirmation on Sunday!"

They walked to Sharie's house. "Should we do our thing?" Gina asked Sharie.

"Yes! Always!"

They reached Sharie's house and walked past it. Sharie walked Gina all the way home. Then Gina walked her halfway back. They parted in the middle. Both ran home as fast as they could.

7

—————

Gina awakened early. She had one worry on her mind. She thought, "Dad knows when my Confirmation is. What if he shows up? I don't want him there." Putting on a robe, she considered again. "There's no way he would come to it. It's a Sunday morning. He played music last night. He's in bed."

She went downstairs to breakfast. Lily was sitting at the table and smiling. There were a beautiful card and six roses near her cocoa and toast. She looked at the card. On the cover was a white dove illuminated by white light. Gina opened the card.

> Oh, Spirit
> Descend into my heart
> I will enlighten the dark corners of
> my life
> And scatter cheerful beams

"Mom, that's beautiful. Thank you! And our house needs cheering up. You wrote a wonderful poem."

"I didn't exactly write it. Here's the one St. Augustine wrote. I messed with it a little."

Gina read from the piece of paper Lily gave her.

> Oh, Holy Ghost
> Descend plentifully into my heart
> Enter the dark corners of this ne-
> glected dwelling
> And scatter thy cheerful beams.

> - St. Augustine

Gina said, "It sounds like I have dark corners. Like I'm a ramshackle old house. And 'Holy Ghost' always sounds weird. Plus it sounds like the Holy Ghost does everything to make things better. I want to make them better by myself."

"I agree. That's why I changed it. I have something else for you." She handed Gina a large flat box. It was wrapped in flowered paper that Lily had painted.

Gina opened the box. She took out a pale cream colored long dress. The fabric was covered with pale blue and cornflower blue flowers and green leaves.

"Mom, there isn't a tag. Did you make this for me?" she asked. She held it up to herself.

"I did. I used the sewing machine in the scene shop at the theater where I perform. Do you like it?" Lily asked.

"I love it!" Gina assured her.

"It's based on a dress from *Sense and Sensibility* by Jane Austen. There is a copy of the book under the tissue. One of the girls in it reminds me of you."

"Which one? Does she get confirmed?" Gina asked.

"No, she realizes something about herself. It doesn't have anything to do with religion, only spirit," Lily explained.

"Perfect present! I'll read the book later. I'm going to go put on my dress!"

As Gina dressed, she thought about the dove

she saw in church. She saw the dove when she was very little.

"Not a real dove," she remembered. "But I saw something. I was four and we were at the Cathedral. I looked up at some lights over the altar. The lights formed a dove. Whenever I went back I looked for it, but I never saw it again."

She put on white shoes. She brushed her long hair. Lily came in. She pinned some fresh Lilies of the Valley in Gina's hair.

"Are we allowed to wear flowers?" Gina asked.

"Well, you're allowed to wear veils and scarves on your head in church. These days you don't have to. It's a choice. I figured we'd choose for you to wear flowers.

"Why Lilies of the Valley?"

Lily explained, "They are a symbol of joy, love, happiness, and luck. Remember your First Communion? You looked like an angel. You wore a white veil."

"I was dressed like a bride! I remember I looked around. I thought, a bunch of seven year-olds are dressed up like brides and grooms! That is so messed up. Did you know nuns wear wedding rings because they are married to Christ? That is the weirdest," Gina remarked.

Lily continued pinning flowers in Gina's hair. "I know. And so Catholic."

"Okay. I'm ready. Let's go. Do you think dad will show up?"

"I didn't tell him about it. Did you?" Lily asked. She picked up her purse.

"No. I am fine if he's not there."

Gina and Lily walked to Our Lady of Victory. They saw other families walking to church. Everyone was dressed in their best. Lily wore a pale blue linen long dress with a matching jacket. She had made it herself. They waved to families and friends across the street. Gina did not see her father anywhere. She was relieved.

Father Ambrose was on the church steps. He greeted each family. All were seated and music was played. Prayers were read. Finally it was Gina's turn to approach the altar. She knelt on the top step. The bishop anointed her forehead with oil.

Gina took a deep breath. She returned to her seat. She closed her eyes. She thought, "I don't feel anything. No foreign words floated into my head." She opened her eyes. "I thought I was supposed to be able to speak other languages now?" she mused to herself.

She poked Phil. "Did you feel anything?" she whispered.

He answered in Gaelic, "Is dóigh liom rud ar bith. Níl grá ag Dia dom."

She rolled her eyes. "Gaelic?"

A smile flitted across his face. "It means, 'I don't feel anything. God doesn't love me.'"

Gina bowed her head and stifled a laugh. Phil's dad turned around. He glared at them to be quiet.

After the ceremony, they all went over to Phil's house for a party. Lily and Sharie's parents attended. Gina, Sharie, and Phil walked ahead of the parents.

Sharie exclaimed, "I'm mad! Why can't I magically speak another language now? Like Phil with Gaelic? I feel like they lied to us. Speaking in tongues!"

"The Catholic church never promised anything," Phil reminded her.

"Maybe it takes a while to kick in," Gina offered.

"I'm going to make to make up my own language!" Sharie spoke several sentences of gobbledygook.

Gina and Phil copied her. The three walked along laughing. They spoke their own made-up silly language.

They had Phil's mom's Irish apple cake and ice cream Everyone played with the kittens. Lily chatted with Phil and Sharie's parents. Late in the afternoon, Gina and Lily thanked Phil's parents.

Lily said to both sets of parents at the door. "I will make sure Gina stays in touch. Thank you for a lovely party."

They started walking home. "Why are you going to keep me in touch with Sharie and Phil? We hang out all summer," Gina asked.

Lily put a hand on Gina's shoulder. "I was just going to tell you. I'm sorry to tell you this. Sharie is moving to the suburbs. And Phil is moving back to Ireland."

"What?! When?"

"When school is out. Sharie and Phil just found out last night. Their parents asked them not to say anything. They wanted me to break it to you," Lily said.

"Well that's the second and third crummy thing to happen today," Gina complained.

"The second and third? What was the first?" Lily asked. She stopped to smell a rose from a neighbor's rosebush.

"Mom, I know it's silly. A little part of me thought that I would be able to speak other languages after Confirmation."

"That's how religions get you!" Lily secretly

plucked the rose. She gave it to Gina when they were well past the owner's house.

"Mom, that's awful! I suppose you're right. It is how religions get you."

They both burst out laughing and raced the rest of the way home.

8

Gina walked home from school on Monday with Sharie and Phil as usual. Sharie grabbed Gina's hand and swung it. Gina said, "I can't believe you two are moving away."

Sharie said, "At least I'll be in the same state, not like Phil. He won't even be in the same country!"

"It's almost our last time together," Phil added.

Gina looked down. "It will be awful without you guys at school. Phil, why do you have to go back to Ireland again?"

Phil answered, "My parents want to live in Belfast like we used to. The Belfast Agreement was signed last April. Most of the violence of the Troubles is over."

"The Troubles?" Sharie asked.

Phil sighed deeply. "It's really complicated. My family are Irish Republicans. They have been fighting to be the Republic of Ireland. They don't want to be part of the United Kingdom."

"Who are they fighting against?" Gina asked.

"Some of the people who live in Northern Ireland. They want to be part of the United Kingdom. A lot of the fighting has been in Belfast. That's where our house is," Phil explained.

"Why don't you go back to some city that's not Belfast?" Sharie asked.

"My dad says our family has lived in Belfast for centuries. He thinks we all should try to get along. Both sets of my grandparents live there. My uncles, aunts, and cousins live there. I miss them. I could speak Gaelic all the time again."

"I'll miss you," said Gina.

"Me, too! And your parents. I love their Irish accents!" Sharie added.

Phil laughed. "Except you can never understand a word they say."

"It sounds pretty. Why don't you have an accent?" Sharie asked.

"I guess if you come to the U.S. when you're little, you don't have an accent. I was five when I got here. You know, I speak Gaelic at home."

"All the time? You can switch back and forth between English and Gaelic? You should be an actor," Gina told him.

"Mmm... Maybe. Let's talk about something else," Phil requested.

"Let's talk about Jinx! My kitten. When can I take him home from your house?" Sharie asked.

Sharie and Phil chatted about Jinx's new home. Only Gina overheard the three girls walking in front of them.

"Did you hear about Gina's dog? Her dad didn't make sure the door was shut. And the gate was open. The dog ran out into the driveway. Her dad's friend ran over him. Her dad told everyone that the dog was stolen," one of the girls from Gina's English class reported.

One of them said, "Gina should have been more careful with her dog! She can be smart in class, but a total idiot, too! That dog probably didn't even want to live with her."

Another girl frowned. "You know about the all police visits and her mom's black eye. I don't know why Gina and her mom don't leave him."

The third volunteered, "My dad went to high school with Gina's dad. They named him 'Ted the Jerk.' Except they called him 'TJ' so he never knew. He thought it was because he was named after his dad. He was Ted, Jr. Once a loser, always a loser, my mom says."

The girls turned a corner. Gina shook her head. She tried to get the memory of those horrid girls out of her mind.

She pondered, "I hate those girls, except for one thing. I wonder why mom doesn't leave dad?" She had a terrible thought, "She can't because of me! He hardly pays any bills. She doesn't make enough to take care of both of us."

Phil and Sharie stopped at the corner. There were For Sale signs on the front lawns of Phil's and Sharie's houses.

"Bye, you guys. We'll have to have extra fun at the end of the year picnic next week," Gina said.

"Yeah!" Phil and Sharie said a little sadly. "See you tomorrow!"

The ballet barre and large mirror beckoned after dinner. Gina's mother worked tirelessly at her studio teaching ballet. Her life's work was ballet. She taught girls and boys whose parents did not make a lot of money. They would not have been able to study dance, if not for Lily.

"Mom, why aren't you too tired to do ballet with me every day?" Gina asked that evening. She set up the record player. Ballet lessons from her mother were a treasured part of Gina's day. "I love it so much, but it's new for me. You do it all the time."

"Dancing with you is special for me, too. You are so graceful and delicate. Sometimes I can't believe I gave birth to such a beautiful dancer! Besides, I spent most of today writing grants for funding. I sat in a chair so much I'm not tired."

Lily put a leg on the barre. She began a gentle stretch. "Studio rent, insurance, salary for me and the pianist never go away. We're okay, though. My studio is for dancers whose parents can't afford lessons."

Sometimes they watched old ballet movies on the evenings Lily wasn't performing or teaching. This evening they cheered Leslie Brown from the sofa. She danced with Mikhail Baryshnikov in *The Turning Point.*

"I bet Uncle Gene goes to see a lot of ballet. It's huge in Russia, isn't it? I forgot, what is he doing there?" Gina asked.

Lily answered, "He's working on a PhD in Russian language and history. Yes, I suppose he goes to the ballet."

"But we both know he spends way more time in museums and libraries. My uncle, the handsome nerd. Will he ever have a girlfriend that lasts? He goes through a lot of them," Gina said.

"He does. Who knows what he's looking for? All of my girlfriends from school were in love with him. Now all the dancers I know are, female and male. Oh, this is a good part," Lily said pointing to the television screen.

After the movie was over, Lily said, "Gina, I would like you to take ballet class downtown. I have done all I can for you. I'd like you to take lessons from Madame Branitskaya. She was my teacher. She is Russian."

"But, mom I like doing ballet with you! Remember I was mugged on the street selling candy for my old Brownie troop. I don't want to go downtown alone! I thought you said I was too young?" Gina asked.

"Oh, yes. I forgot about that." Lily took Gina's hand. "You have progressed so much. I promise you will be safe. Will you please think about it?"

Gina began to cry. Lily put her arm around her. "Gina, what is it?"

Gina took a deep breath. "Everyone is going away. Dad is horrible. Phil is going back to Ireland. Sharie is moving and going to a new school. Uncle Gene is gone. I won't have you as a ballet teacher. I don't even have Pepe!"

Lily stroked Gina's hair off of her forehead. She said thoughtfully, "Maybe it's not the right time to do this, Gina. I'm sorry. You can still be with me. I love teaching you ballet."

Gina felt slightly better. She looked up at Lily. "I will think about ballet downtown. I'll let you know."

Lily smiled, "Whatever you decide to do is good! Now sleep well. I love you!"

"Love you, too, mom," Gina said heading to her room.

Gina brushed her teeth, put on pajamas, and got into bed. She pulled the covers up to her chin and turned out the light. She wondered, "Could I really take ballet lessons downtown? Maybe I could."

She turned over and fell asleep. She dreamed she was waiting in the wings to go on stage. She wore a tutu and pointe shoes. The orchestra played an overture. She stepped toward the stage. A great light shone in her eyes. It blinded her. A great gust of wind blew her backwards. She fell onto the floor.

She dreamed that other dancers stepped over her as they went on stage to dance. She scrambled to her feet. The dancers had already finished their dance.

Gina awakened. She sat up and leaned on one arm. She reached to pet Pepe. He wasn't there. She cried and cried. "I miss Pepe!"

She pounded her pillow with a fist. "I will never let mean girls bother me again! And I am going to take ballet lessons downtown!" At last, she fell asleep.

9

The following Saturday Gina slept late. Lily came in with cocoa for her. "Gina, wake up. It's late," she said gently.

Gina turned over. "It's not late to me. I had to go to afternoon kindergarten, remember? Because you couldn't get me up."

Lily laughed, "That's true."

"I thought about ballet all week. I decided. I will take ballet lessons downtown with Madame," Gina said, sipping.

"Oh, Gina that is wonderful! I hoped you would!" Lily danced around Gina's tiny room.

"In that case, we are doing something special today. We are going to buy new things for your ballet classes downtown. Madame has very spe-cific requirements."

They went to a shop called Grand Jete'. Young girls and their mothers bought leotards, tights, and ballet slippers there. Some older girls were allowed to buy the hard, pink satin pointe shoes.

"I'll dance in pointe shoes someday? Right, mom?" Gina asked. She was being fitted for flat, pink leather ballet slippers.

"When Madame says that you are old enough and strong enough. Then we can buy pointe shoes," Lily answered.

Lily knew the shop owner somewhat. They chatted about dance performances around the city. "Lily, I hear you will be dancing the role of The Novice in *The Cage*. Are you sure you're up to that? It's a tough part," the petite owner asked with pursed lips. She had been a dancer herself.

Lily made an effort to smile graciously. "I trust my director and choreographer. They chose me. I am giving it my all."

Gina took her mother by the hand. She led her to a display of tights before the owner could say anything else. "Mom, is this the kind I need?" Gina asked. Then she whispered, "Why do people have to be so horrible? Of course you will be great in *The Cage*."

Lily smiled gratefully. She whispered back, "I don't know. I would never talk to anyone the way the shop owner talked to me."

The night before her first lesson Gina couldn't sleep at all. She imagined she was frozen in a class with other little girls. "I know they all will be perfect. They will have perfect lives. Their families tell them how great they are all the time. I don't belong with them! I don't belong anywhere, except at home."

Lily came into Gina's room in the morning. Her daughter lay flat on her back. She stared at the ceiling with wide open eyes. "It's okay, Gina. I didn't sleep before my first lesson, either."

Gina sat up in bed and Lily hugged her. "I promise it will be okay."

Gina slowly began to dress, "What if it's not?"

Lily handed her a clean blouse. "Then we will try again on a different day. Ballet is already a part of your life. We will figure it out. Remember to call Madame Branitskaya, 'Madame.'"

"Okay. I have my dance bag. I'm glad we packed it last night. I'm too nervous to think about what should be in it," Gina said.

"Check it again anyway. I'll start the car."

Gina zipped it open. She realized she hadn't packed one of the new ballet shoes. "Mom, was right!" She found it under the bed and popped it into the bag. Closing it again, she ran to the kitchen. She stepped outside, locked the door, and got into the car.

"Why aren't we taking the bus?" Gina wondered.

"Because it's a special day," Lily said. She adjusted the volume on the radio.

Lily drove around downtown for a while looking for a parking spot. Lily finally found an open meter. They walked a few blocks and entered the old red stone building. They crossed the marble-floored lobby to the elevator. Gina looked at the directory. Her eyes flicked past offices on the first few floors.

Lily pointed to the ballet school. It was on floors three through six. On floors seven and eight there was a theatre that produced works by new playwrights. The doors opened. Lily pressed the button. She chose the fourth floor.

"Mothers don't watch, Gina. It's a professional school. After we check you in, I'll show you where to change and put your things."

"Oh, okay." Gina looked up. Lily was smiling down at her.

They stepped off the elevator. Lily approached a high wooden desk. The reception area was surrounded by large windows looking out over high-rises, department stores, restaurants, and hotels. A young woman found Gina's name in a book. She made a mark next to her name. Lily thanked her and led Gina down the hall. They passed a drinking fountain and went into a room with lockers and long wooden benches.

Lily helped Gina change into pink tights, a black leotard and pink leather ballet shoes. Gina's hair was already in a bun. Lily had put her hair up for her before they left home. Lily had told Gina, "Next time, you will put your hair up on your own."

Gina put her street clothes and dance bag in a locker. She locked it using the lock Lily had given her. She tucked the key into the sleeve of her leotard. Lily had sewed a special pocket in her leotard for the key. They were alone in the dressing room. Lily had insisted that they arrive early.

They went back into the hallway. There were many girls and a few boys arriving with parents. Lily showed Gina into the studio. One entire wall was covered from floor to ceiling with mirrors. There were ballet barres on all of the walls.

Lily was careful not to step on the dance floor in her outdoor shoes. She pointed out where Gina should stand. Gina stepped up onto the sprung dance floor. She took her place. She looked back at Lily. "Sit down on the floor and stretch until Madame arrives. I will see you in an hour and a half," Lily said.

Gina nodded and did as Lily directed. A pianist arrived. She adjusted her seat before sitting down and opened her music. Madame entered and smiled at Gina. Other girls came in and took places at the barres around the room.

Madame announced in her strong Ukrainian accent, "Foot and ankle warm up, facing barre. Lydia, please play." The pianist played. The lesson began.

Gina drew a short breath. She placed both hands on the barre. She faced the barre and the mirror. She looked into her green eyes. She thought, "This is exactly the right place for me."

Her mother had taught the foot and ankle warm up to her at home. Now she did it along with live music for the first time. She nervously thought to herself, "It feels good to be in this huge room. I love the high ceilings and the mirrors."

She completed the exercise. Madame gave instructions to perform the next exercise. Gina placed her left hand on the barre. She faced sideways from the mirror. Lydia played the first few bars of music on the piano. The students began the exercise together.

"I feel safe here," Gina thought. "I like being in a big, stone and marble building. I am here with Madame. Nothing can hurt me. I don't have allergies here. I can breathe." Her thoughts continued. "And the music, the piano, it is so wonderful."

Gina completed each exercise carefully. She remembered the sequence of steps as soon as Madame demonstrated them. At the end of class she performed "reverence" along with the other students. The young dancers stood in rows in the room and curtsied, first to the right, and then to the left. They did this to thank Madame. The boys bowed from the waist.

After class, Gina took the key out of the special pocket in her leotard. She unlocked her locker and changed back into street clothes. She crammed her sweaty dance clothes and shoes into her bag. She found Lily waiting in the lobby for her. Lily was writing furiously in a notebook.

"Mom, it was good! What are you writing?"

Lily kissed her on the top of her head. She gathered her things to go. "Today is about you. I'll tell you later. Tell me everything about the class!"

The two chatted in the elevator, out onto the street and getting into the car. They continued talking on the car ride, and during the walk from the garage to the house. Once in the kitchen, Lily made tea and they had cookies.

Gina disappeared after dinner. She put Debussy's *Afternoon of a Faun* on the stereo. First, she cried. She always cried when Lily played the record. The music was so beautiful to Gina. Then she stood in front of her full length mirror. She made slow, graceful movements with her arms.

She felt as though she had been given the most amazing present of grace and lightness. She kept that feeling within herself long after she had fallen asleep.

10

Lily rode the bus with Gina over the next few weeks to ballet classes. Lily waited nervously in the lobby for Gina to finish her lesson. She hustled her out and back onto the bus.

"Mom, I know you have things you could be doing while I am at ballet class," Gina commented one evening. They crossed the busy street to walk to the bus stop.

Lily sighed wearily. "You are right. You know, one of the windows in the studio overlooks the busy street you have to cross. Maybe Madame could watch you from the window."

"She teaches the class after mine. I have a better idea. Do you remember Madame's son?" Gina asked.

"Mischa? He's just a little boy?"

"Not any more. He's a teenager. He's studying photography. He comes to the studio every time I take class. I think he likes a girl, Ashley, in the later class. He might help us," Gina suggested.

"Excellent! And I think Ashley will be quite impressed that he helps out a little girl between classes. I'll call Madame."

The next time Gina had a lesson, Madame entered the studio. Gina quickly turned to curtsey.

"Gina, my son will walk you to bus stop after class. All time. It is his new job."

"Thank you, Madame! You and Mischa are very kind."

"Gina, about pirouettes. I will tell secret. Pretend to be screwing self into floor when making pirouette. Now show."

Gina imagined there was a power drill on her foot. She tried screwing her pirouette into the floor with her mind. She looked even jerkier and clumsier.

"Hmm...," Madame said. "Think that there is string attached to top of head. Someone in ceiling is pulling you upward in pirouette."

Gina tried and stumbled.

Madame sighed. "It is okay. Do not scare. It is

pirouette! Easy step. Work at home," she advised. She waved the other students into the room.

After class, Mischa dutifully escorted Gina to the bus stop. Gina felt quite pleased to have an older boy make sure she was safe. He was tall and slender, and very handsome. He chatted about photography. He spoke with a charming Ukrainian accent like Madame's.

"I need to show world as different, not as people usually see." He stopped on the sidewalk and lay down on his back.

"Mischa, what are you doing?" Gina asked in shock.

He snapped a photo of the tall buildings surrounding them. He got up and explained. "With this photo I can show how it feels to be small. We are so small compared to the buildings. We do not think of this as we are walking in the city."

"I guess not. This is my stop. There are always people here. It's okay."

Mischa looked around. "This seems safe. This tobacco store is open late. Go in there and call Madame if anyone bothers you. I will come." He bounded off, anxious to get back to the ballet class to photograph Ashley.

Gina waited for her bus alone in front of a department store. Gina nodded to a black middle aged woman. She was always on the bus stop with Gina at that time. Gina thought, "She is so beautiful. Tall and slender with cheekbones. I wonder if she modeled when she was younger?"

"How are you doing? You are alone tonight. Is everything all right?" the woman asked.

Gina smiled. She answered, "Yes. My mother can't wait with me. My ballet teacher's son walked me here from the dance academy. I am fine, thank you."

"In that case I will keep an eye out for you until your bus comes. My bus comes just after yours. I am Mrs. Adams," she smiled back.

"I'm Gina. Thank you for waiting with me," Gina said politely.

And so, week after week, Mrs. Adams waited with her. "When you get off the bus, run!" Mrs. Adams always told Gina as she boarded her bus.

Gina smiled back. She prepared herself to run as soon as the bus stopped. She moved toward the front of the bus. She had the house key in her hand and firmly clutched the handles of her dance bag.

At her stop, she thanked the bus driver and stepped off. She started running. She saw lights on in Mrs. Lane's and Mrs. Lemieux's houses. She knew that they were keeping an eye out for her.

Her house was brightly lit as she put her key in the lock.

Lily greeted her at the door.

"Mom, a woman named Mrs. Adams waits with me for the bus," Gina breathlessly told Lily.

"Oh, yes. I remember seeing her. That's wonderful!"

Lily answered the ringing phone. "Yes, Madame. Oh, no. It is fine. I am so thankful that Gina can study with you. And please thank Mischa for me. After he drops Gina she waits with woman named Mrs. Adams for the bus."

"What did Madame want?" Gina asked. She set down her dance bag.

"Only that you are doing very well. But, you started too late this year to be in the recital. Are you disappointed?"

"No! That's great news!" Gina danced around the tiny kitchen. "I don't have to worry about screwing it up anymore!"

11

School passed quickly the next day. It was the last day of sixth grade. Everyone went to mass in the morning. Then students made the rounds of their classes to pick up reports from each teacher. Actual report cards would be mailed home.

The students changed into shorts and tee shirts. They all were going to a picnic in the park surrounding Minnehaha Falls. Then it was time to get on the bus.

Gina, Phil, and Sharie sat together on the bus. They squeezed into one seat. They sang and laughed. Soon the bus pulled into the parking lot for the falls. Once off of the bus, the three raced to the falls.

Sharie lifted her chin. "I can feel the water spray on my face!" she exclaimed.

Phil snapped a photo of the two girls in front of the falls. They had their arms around each other's waists. "The falls are really powerful. It must be because of all the rain we had. Wow," Phil whistled. "Hey, they're starting the Cake Walk! Let's go over there. I want to try to win my mom's Irish apple cake."

"Why doesn't she make some for you at home?" Gina asked. She skipped alongside them.

"It's only for holidays. Or for when she wants to show off, like when she makes a cake for school," he explained.

Gina and Sharie played in the Cake Walk along with Phil. They promised that they would give him the cake if they won. The music stopped. Gina stood behind the chair closest to her. She won the cake. It was beautiful. The three went to a picnic table. They cut slices for themselves, leaving plenty for Phil for later.

Gina took a bite. "It is the best cake I have ever had. The slices of apple in the middle are perfect, and the cream topping. Yum!"

Phil and Sharie nodded, happily munching.

Sharie nudged Phil. She said, "Gina, we have to go to the Telegram Booth. It's new this year."

Gina licked whipped cream off of a finger. "What is it?"

They giggled and ran off, "You'll see!"

Ahead of her, Gina saw Sharie quickly give a note to Linda. She was running the Telegram Booth. Phil tried to shield Sharie and Linda from Gina's view.

"What are you guys up to?" Gina asked. She came up behind them, puffing.

"Nothing!" the three said in chorus.

Phil grabbed Gina's arm. "Come on! To the campfire. It's time for lunch."

"But what does the Telegram Booth do?!" Gina asked.

Sharie and Phil both hurried Gina toward the picnic tables by the fire pit. They pestered her with questions. "Gina, do you want a burger or a hot-dog? Ketchup? Mustard? Both? How about a pop? What kind?"

"What's wrong with you guys? I can get my own stuff," Gina said. She joined the hotdog line.

They met back at a picnic table. The three tried not to talk about Phil leaving. Sharie ran off to get cupcakes for them. She returned just as one of the eighth graders arrived. He climbed up onto their table. He was wearing a tee shirt with *Telegram Delivery* written on it.

He unrolled a piece of paper. He read aloud to the whole school. In a rather booming voice for a fourteen year old boy, he announced, "Dear Gina, You have been elected to be patrol captain for next year. You're so pretty all the cars want to stop for you anyway. I'll still be a patrol if you want me on your team. P.S. I like you, Tim."

Students of all grades whooped and cheered and clapped. Gina turned all the shades of red that exist. Sister Margaret Mary came over to the table. She gave Gina the head patrol badge to keep over the summer.

The Telegram Delivery boy asked Gina, "What would you like to say in a telegram in response?"

Gina stuttered, "Say that I am happy to be the captain next year."

Phil shouted, "And put in that Gina likes Tim, too!"

Gina hid her face in a napkin, laughing. She didn't try to stop the Telegram Delivery boy from writing that last bit on the telegram.

Sharie, Phil, and Gina played Frisbee after the picnic. Tim approached. Gina turned to her two friends, "Don't you dare tease us!"

Sharie and Phil shrieked, "Us! She said 'us'!"

They laughed. Phil tossed the Frisbee into the

woods. Then he grabbed Sharie's hand to go find it with him.

Gina turned to Tim. She said, "You are such a geek. You nominated me for captain because you know I will let you go early for baseball practice."

"Well, yeah," he smiled.

Gina put her hand out, "Okay, deal." And they shook on it.

She thought, "That was sort of like holding hands with him for the first time."

In the late afternoon they tossed frisbees around. They ate ice cream. When the sun was dipping, they all climbed back onto the bus. Gina was sunburned and covered with mosquito bites. She was tired and happy.

Gina let Tim sit with her on the way back. Sharie and Phil were behind them. Sharie kept kicking the back of Gina's seat. Gina refused to give in and turn around. She paid Sharie no attention at all. The driver let them off at school. Gina waved "Good-Bye" to Tim. She and Sharie and Phil set off for their homes.

The three passed Phil's house and walked to Sharie's. Then they walked to Gina's. Gina walked with them back half way to Sharie's. They hugged all together.

"I'll miss you guys," Gina said. Her voice was muffled by Phil's shoulder.

"I'll miss you!" Sharie sniffled. "We are moving tomorrow. Gina we can still see each other. It's dumb old Phil who has to leave forever."

Phil stepped back a little. He looked at the girls. "Ireland is not the moon. You could come there to see me, you know. Why did I have to walk Gina home? And now Sharie? We went by my house first."

"It's payment for letting you hang out with us," Sharie said. She patted him on the back.

"It is, Phil. Well, my mom is waiting for me. I'm going to go," Gina said. She disentangled herself from the hug. She walked backward to her house so she could see Sharie and Phil as long as possible. Sharie and Phil walked backward so they could see Gina.

Sharie and Phil fought over who would carry Phil's Irish apple cake. Phil tripped and fell. Sharie had to help him up. He mimed having broken his leg to make the girls laugh. They turned the corner. Gina ran the rest of the way home.

Gina came into the house. Lily had an antihistamine ready. "Take this for the bug bites. Your skin is already swelling. They really love you," she said. She put a cream on the bites. "How was it?"

"It was good and bad. Tim finally admitted he likes me," Gina said. She swallowed the antihistamine.

"I knew he would. I'm thinking that is the good thing?" Lily asked.

"Yes. And the bad thing is Phil and Sharie going away. It's so awful."

"I was thinking of that. I can help you and Sharie get together sometimes. Going to see Phil would take a lot of money. Maybe we can go someday," Lily offered.

"It's okay for now, mom."

"How are the girls in your ballet classes with Madame? Could any of them be your friends?" Lily asked.

"Oh, you know. The girls are into themselves and boys and clothes and make-up. Dumb stuff," Gina said.

"I remember well. Sometimes it takes time. You will find a friend in dance. I'm sure."

"Hmm. That would be nice. Dance is a lot all on its own, though, mom"

"It is," Lily agreed.

"I think ballet is life's big band-aid. Madame says it's addictive."

"Madame said that? Well, I guess it's true," Lily laughed. "But, a healthy addiction. Let's watch something Disney tonight. *The Little Mermaid*?"

"Perfect! It's summer and Ariel is in the ocean. Oh, and she learns to walk and I'm learning how to dance! Wish I had a hot Prince Eric, though. Tim will have to do for now," Gina giggled.

"Just because in fairy tales the characters always get married..." Lily warned.

Gina interrupted, "Marry Tim? No way! He'd wear a baseball uniform instead of a tux to the wedding!"

"We can't have bad costuming," Lily laughed. She settled on the sofa.

"The costuming is the only weird thing about the *Little Mermaid*. That shell bra she wears looks really uncomfortable," Gina said.

Lily got up and took two teacups out of the china closet. She put them over her chest. "Yep, this is awful!"

Gina grabbed two more teacups. She held them over her chest. She laughed. "It's too funny," Gina said. She set them on the coffee table. "Come on, let's watch the movie. We can dance and sing to all the songs."

Lily went to the kitchen. She returned with tea to put in the cups. The Disney castle appeared on the screen.

12

———

Now Gina took the bus alone to ballet class. She knew exactly where to get off and how to walk to the arts building. On this day, it was early afternoon. It was warm and sunny, but windy. Gina was small and slender. The wind was so strong it pushed her along. She smiled, "The universe especially wants me to get to ballet class today."

She hurried into dance clothes. Before anyone else was there, she entered the studio. "I am going to do pirouettes. I mean practice trying to do pirouettes. I'm awful at them!" she thought. She looked into her eyes in the mirror to spot her clumsy turns. "I can barely make it around once. Madame wants doubles!"

Gina noticed a group of three girls entering the

studio. She stopped quickly and began a stretch on the floor. The girls moved together. They took their usual places at the barre. They called themselves the Three Ballerinateers. Gina did not bother to greet them. They neither looked at her, or talked to her.

Lydia came in and nodded to Gina. She wound her piano stool to the proper height and sat down. She opened her music. Madame entered.

Gina loved Madame. Madame always wore black loose pants and a black embroidered blouse. Even so, in Gina's mind she was in full costume, bodice, tutu, pointe shoes, and feathers in her hair.

Gina rose to curtsey. The Ballerinateers remained on the floor stretching. One called out to Madame. "The Three Ballerinateers are ready for their lesson, Madame."

Madame and Lydia were facing Gina. The trio of girls could not see Madame's and Lydia's faces. Gina saw Madame and Lydia roll their eyes at each other.

Madame came over to Gina. She whispered, "We conquer pirouettes today. More important than being like other girls."

Gina smiled and relaxed. She didn't turn a single proper pirouette. Gina didn't care. Madame liked her. She floated through the class. She curtsied to Madame at the end of class. The Ballerina-teers clapped enthusiastically for Madame.

Madame told the class, "In Russia we do not clap in studio. Only for theater. Clapping is American. But, I accept this from you."

One of the Ballerinateers said, "Madame, dancers in New York clap for their teacher at the end of class. Don't you want to be like a New York ballet teacher?"

"I do not. Russian method is best." Madame gave the girl a cold stare. Then she swept out of the room.

Gina changed clothes quickly. The other girls in the dressing room chatted and primped in the mirror. Gina thought, "I wonder if I will ever study ballet in Russia? Wouldn't that be wonderful?"

Gina's bus home passed through downtown by stores and apartments. She thought some more. "Uncle Gene is in Russia. Maybe I could stay with him and study ballet. I can't even imagine going to Ireland to see Phil. How would I get to Russia? Russia is too scary. Uncle Gene should add a Russian ballerina to his list of girlfriends. She could write to me. She could tell me what it's like to be a ballerina there."

Gina smiled. She thought of dancing in her first pair of pointe shoes. "If I ever get them!

Madame told me I'm not strong enough to study on pointe," she thought. She looked out the window.

"I'll just get older and stronger!" Gina resolved.

At home she went into the kitchen. Lily handed her an envelope. "Gina, you have a letter! How was class?"

"Class was great. No pirouettes yet. That's okay," Gina said sitting down. "Thanks for making cookies!"

She took a cookie from the plate on the table. She opened the letter. It was from Uncle Gene.

June 1, 1989

Dear Gina,

Your mother wrote me that you are studying ballet downtown with Madame Branitskaya. She was your mother's teacher. She loved Lily and she will love you, too. That is truly wonderful. You will be a lovely ballerina. As Carl Jung famously said, "Nothing affects a child's life more than the life of the parent."

Gina thought for a moment. "What does that mean? Mom is a dancer. Do I want to dance just because mom does? Do I want to be better at it than she is? And who is Carl Jung? I never understand Uncle Gene."

I often go to the ballet here in Russia. I hope you and Lily will see the Kirov Theatre someday. It is beautiful, pale aqua and white on the outside. The interior is decorated with white marble sculptures, gold chandeliers, and mirrors. It was built many years ago in 1783.

Gina looked up momentarily. "He is so wordy. And always, history, history. I do kind of like it, though."

I miss you and your mother. I am busy here with my studies. Soon I will have a PhD. I will come back to Minnesota to look for a job teaching Russian and Russian Studies. Too boring for you now, but when you are older you might be interested in what I do.

It is wonderful to study the languages of other people. Maybe you will try it someday. I will be in Minneapolis soon for a visit.

Do you remember in 1987 President Ronald Reagan challenged Mikhail Gorbachev to tear down the Berlin Wall? It is a wall that prevents people living in Communist East Germany from ever leaving. The East Germans have little freedom in their lives. Soon they might have more freedom. It is a very exciting time to be in Russia!

Love, Uncle Gene

. . .

"Does he really think I remember President Reagan saying that? I was eight years old. I don't understand why people are kept behind a wall. I'm sure he will explain it to me for a long time when I see him! Well, I'm glad he's happy. I miss him," she thought.

Gina looked over at Lily. "What is that notebook you are scribbling in? Your diary?"

"I am writing a story so that I can better understand *The Cage.* I have to dance a main part. I need to understand the story better. So, I am rewriting it in my own way. It helps," Lily explained.

"What is *The Cage* about?" Gina wondered.

"I honestly can't decide if you're old enough to know," Lily sighed.

"As long as you are writing, mom. I will write to Uncle Gene."

Gina took out paper and pencil and began.

June 10, 1989

Dear Uncle Gene,

How are you? I am fine. I think you should find a Russian ballerina girlfriend. Wouldn't that be fun? Then you wouldn't have to go to the library all the time.

I am starting summer ballet classes tomorrow. I

will be in the dance studio five hours every day for six weeks! Not on Saturday and Sunday. We don't dance on those days.

I will have a ballet lesson from ten to eleven thirty. From eleven thirty to noon I will be in pointe class. I am not yet allowed to dance in pointe shoes. Madame said I am not strong enough yet. In pointe class I will do everything on tip-toe in leather ballet slippers. Mom says Madame put me in pointe class because I will start wearing pointe shoes soon. I can't wait to get pointe shoes!

Then we will have lunch. After that we will have a folk dancing class and a special class for pirouettes. The last class will be jumping. That's the hardest one. The boys are best at jumping. I think there will be four boys in class. And many girls.

I think it will be okay. I can't turn pirouettes hardly at all. I hope the pirouette class helps. I love to jump, but I look awful doing it.

I don't remember about President Reagan and the wall thing. You can explain it all to me when I see you. I understand that people in some countries have mean, horrible leaders. Please don't get close to those mean leaders!

Love, Gina

13

───────────

Gina drank cocoa the following morning. Today was her first day of summer ballet lessons. She packed a dance bag, including the lunch Lily made for her. Lily walked her to the bus stop. It was a beautiful day, sunny and warm. Birds were singing. Children laughed and splashed in the kiddie pool in the park across from the bus stop.

"Don't worry if you get tired. It's a long day of dancing for you. Drink water, but not too much. It will weigh you down. Sips every hour or so. Drink a lot of water at the end of the day. There is a back lobby on first floor of the building with easy chairs. You can have lunch there if you like. Or, find a bench on the Nicollet Mall."

"Mom, I will be okay." Gina hugged Lily. She

climbed onto the bus. She waved at Lily as they pulled away.

Gina got off the elevator and went into the lobby. Mothers and their children swarmed. The mothers pinned up their daughters hair and fussed over them. The mothers smiled stiffly. They were waiting to find out what level their children were placed in. One of the younger teachers announced the names in each level. She started with the lowest level and worked up to the highest level. Some mothers frowned and left. They found out their daughters were to spend the summer in a low level.

Gina had a surprise waiting for her. Madame had placed her in the first grouping. Gina would be with advanced, older dancers. She went to the dressing room and changed. She locked her bag and clothes in her locker. She made her way to the largest studio with the rest of her level.

She asked Madame politely, "Madame, why am I here? I wasn't even in the recital. I'm not on pointe yet. The other girls in this class are all on pointe."

"It is where you belong. Pointe will come soon. Remember, performance comes last for ballerina," Madame told her.

Gina thought with pride, "That was the first time Madame ever called me a ballerina!"

The other girls ignored her. No one was friendly. Gina decided she didn't care. She sat down to stretch. The class was difficult. Gina didn't know some of the steps. She gritted her teeth during a tough jumping combination. She thought, "Madame says this is where I belong. I hope she's right!"

At the beginning of pointe class Gina sat and watched. The girls put tape on their toes to protect them. They stuffed lamb's wool in the tips of their shoes. Finally, they put the shoes on. They wound pink ribbons around their ankles. Each girl tied the ribbons in a square knot on the inside of her ankle. That way the audience wouldn't see the knot so well.

No one looked at Gina or talked to her. She relaxed and took her place at the barre with them.

"No one cares that I am here. I can relax," she thought.

The girls performed warm up exercise at the barre for quite a while. Gina performed all of the exercises on half pointe. She rose only up to the balls of her feet. The girls in pointe shoe did the exercises on full pointe, rising to the very ends of their toes.

Then the dancers moved into the center of the room. They no longer had a barre to hold onto. The girls on pointe did not look graceful at all. They tried to do everything Madame asked them to do. Some wobbled on pointe and some slipped. The ones who fell quickly scrambled back to their feet.

Gina studied the girls on pointe. She learned many things in the pointe class. Things she would use later, when she finally had her own pointe shoes.

The other girls and boys broke up into little groups at lunch. Their parents had given them money. They went to the fast food restaurants downtown for lunch. Gina took her lunch to the back lobby on first floor that Lily told her about. Lydia, the pianist, was there having her lunch.

"Gina, dear, come sit."

Like Madame, she spoke with a Ukrainian accent. Gina joined her. She tore in to her lunch. She was hungry.

"Gina, you dance well. Don't think about other girls. Have courage."

"Thank you, Lydia." Gina said between mouthfuls. "Today is tough."

"It will be better tomorrow. Have a little coffee."

She poured some from a thermos into a paper

cup for Gina. "Drink coffee an hour before you need it. It will bring you energy. But, not too much." Lydia gathered her things. "I must go to Madame and discuss music for afternoon."

Gina sipped the coffee. She thought, "Ballet has a lot to do with beverages. When to drink them, when not to, how much, how little. It's weird."

The day finished with folk dancing, pirouettes, and jumps and leaps. The girls wore special shoes with heels on them for folk dancing. It was fun for Gina. The others seemed to enjoy themselves, too. Pirouette class was torture, but Gina survived.

"Will I ever be able to turn pretty pirouettes?" she wondered.

The jumping and leaping class was worst of all. Madame saved it for the last class of the day. Jumping and leaping would build strength in tired muscles. The girls were tired, but not the boys. They jumped and leaped as though on springs, with endless energy.

Final curtsies and bows were made to Madame. Gina changed into shorts and a short sleeved blouse. She walked to the bus stop. It was nice to be back out in the sunshine. She sighed deeply on the bus and was tired to her bones.

When she reached home, Lily was waiting for

her. "How was it? Did you have fun? What level are you in? Are there any boys? Do they jump the best?"

"Mom! It was okay. I mostly had fun. I'm in a level with girls who are on pointe. There are maybe four boys. The boys jump the best."

She curled up on the sofa and had a cookie. Lily sipped iced tea.

"What are the other girls like?" Lily asked.

"The girls are boring. Some are okay. Some are horrible. Like they've never had to do dishes or take out the garbage. They are driven from place to place by their mothers. They don't seem very happy. Their mothers don't either. And there are some girls who don't seem real. I don't know. They are sweet and smiling. Like nothing bad has ever happened to them their whole lives. Or, even if it did, they would pretend it was okay," Gina explained.

"That's pretty much what they are like," Lily sighed. "But, the classes are okay?"

"Yes, mom. It's great. I'm just tired."

After dinner Gina bathed. She nodded off to sleep very early in the evening. She finished out her first week of dancing. Lydia was right. It was better every day.

Saturday was bright and sunny. Gina stretched

and got out of bed. She made her way to the kitchen. Cocoa and toast were there waiting for her. Lily poured juice and set it on the table.

"Mom, is it okay that Lydia gives me a little coffee every day at lunch?"

"I don't see a problem with that. I will get you a small thermos. Let's go see Uncle Gene's new place today."

"He's here!? Where is his apartment?"

"He arrived last night. His apartment is on the upper floor of a duplex nearby. His landlady is Russian, so he can keep learning Russian."

Gina rolled her eyes. "He never stops, does he?"

"No. That's my brother."

Gene answered the door immediately. He showed them into a bright living room with windows on two walls. There was a fireplace, cushioned chairs, and a sofa.

"The kitchen is small."

"But, you won't be using it anyway," Lily reminded him.

"Not much. Bella Popova, my landlady has generously offered to cook."

"Young, beautiful widow?" Gina asked.

"Not so much," Gene answered.

Just then a round, dimpled, tiny older woman appeared on the back staircase that led into the kitchen. "Yevgeny, dlya tebya," she said in Russian. She repeated in accented English, "Gene, for you." She handed him a casserole filled with cabbage rolls.

"Thank you! Spasibo! Sistra, Lily, ee doch sistri, Gina," Gene said, introducing Lily and Gina. Bella smiled warmly and left.

"She brings me dinners. And I introduced the two of you," Gene explained.

"We figured that," Lily said. "This looks fantastic. Does she have a daughter?" Lily asked. She put the casserole in the refrigerator.

"I know how your mind works. No. And I am good being single. Besides, I am going back to Russia in a few months."

"Uncle Gene, you are totally missing the eighties," Gina laughed.

"That may be. Let's go to the Institute of Arts. There's a new exhibit."

"Always something educational! Do you ever have fun?" Gina said taking his hand.

"Museums are fun," Lily reminded Gina.

"I know. I like to tease Uncle Gene. Let's go!"

Gina loved going to the art museum. They visited her favorite painting. *Springtime of Life.* It showed a young girl with her hair pinned up in the middle of a forest holding flowers. Jean Baptiste Camille Corot painted it. They visited John Singer Sargent's *Madame X.* She wore an elegant black velvet gown.

Last they visited the mummy of Lady Tashat in the Egyptian collection. They looked through the glass covering at Lady Tashat. They noticed a second skull in her coffin.

Gina read the plaque posted above her. "Lady Tashat was the daughter of a treasurer of the Temple in Egypt. She lived between 1085 and 710 B.C. At the time of her death she was married and about fifteen years old."

Gina looked at Lily. "Married at fifteen? How awful!"

"People didn't live to be as old as they do now. They married much younger," Lily explained.

"Who belongs to the second skull?" Gina asked.

Lily read, "The second skull is a grown man's. It was placed near the legs of Lady Tashat's mummy. Both died violent deaths. Lady Tashat has broken bones and cracked ribs. The back of the man's skull had been beaten in."

"Creepy. A mystery! I wonder what happened? What exhibit are we going to see?" Gina asked.

"It is called *The Shape of Time: Korean Art.* Korea is shifting from dictatorship to democracy," Gene told her.

Gina nodded. "Okay, democracy is everybody gets to vote. And a dictatorship is when one guy tells everyone what to do. And he doesn't let anyone have any freedom."

"Pretty much," Lily nodded.

"Gina, do you know about Tiananmen Square?" Gene asked.

"We talked about it a little in school. It happened right before we got out for the summer. I think you are going to tell me more, though. I know it was tragic," Gina answered.

Gene explained as they walked. "Last June students were demonstrating in Tiananmen Square in Beijing, China. The students wanted democracy, freedom of the press, and freedom of speech. About a million people demonstrated in the square."

The three passed through the rest of the Egyptian collection. They walked on into Greek sculpture.

"The Chinese government sent in troops to occupy the square. Several thousand students and soldiers were killed. Thousands more were wounded," Gene explained.

"All so they could vote and say and write whatever they wanted?" Gina asked in surprise.

"Some people in other countries die for the right to vote," Lily said.

"The world is crazy," Gina remarked.

"It is. The good news is South Korea. They have more freedoms, more money, and more power now." Gene led them into the exhibition hall.

They looked at sculpture, photography, and paintings. The artists created works about their new freedoms and new lives.

"So, new freedoms. Why are there photographs about stress and anxiety? Aren't they happy?" Gina asked, pointing at a photograph.

"I think they are stressed because South Koreans are living side by side with North Korea," Gene explained.

"And they are afraid the North Koreans will come in and take over?" Gina asked.

"Probably," Lily said. She pointed to photographs of young, stressed South Koreans.

Gene added, "Because the world is learning more about South Korea, their faces are seen. Some people don't like how South Koreans look, the shape of their eyes, the color of their skin."

"That's stupid," Gina said. She looked at the young people in the photos. "They're beautiful."

"Parents pressure their children to earn perfect

grades in school. The children are expected to have high paying careers," Gene said. He led them out of the museum into the parking ramp.

"I suppose money is important. But it's sad the parents make the children get perfect grades. The museum was interesting, Uncle Gene," Gina said climbing into the car. "Pizza?"

"Definitely," Lily said with a smile. Gene grinned and eased the car onto the street.

14

Gina finished her first month of summer lessons. She was tired and happy. As she rode her bus home, she felt good about ballet. After getting out at her stop, Gina walked through the neighborhood. There was the scent of summer flowers and she heard the sounds of bees buzzing and birds.

She entered the kitchen. It was unusual for her father to be there on a Thursday in the early evening, but there he was. Gina looked uncertainly from Lily to Ted. Lily stood with her hands on her hips in the middle of the room. Her father sat in a kitchen chair. He looked as though he were trying to make himself smaller.

"So, Gina, your mom tells me you need more money for ballet lessons. What do you think about that?" he asked. He looked at Gina with bleary eyes.

"I, I don't know. If you could, that would be nice. I have been invited to take class every day starting in the fall," Gina's voice faltered.

She turned to Lily, "Maybe we could ask Uncle Gene instead? Or, grandma and grandpa? Or, I could babysit somewhere."

"You are too young to babysit in this neighborhood. It's too dangerous," Lily insisted.

Her father swung his head around to look at Lily. "Oh, now you hate the neighborhood. Is that it?"

Gina shifted from one foot to the other uncertainly. "Maybe you could ask Uncle Gene for some money?"

Her father turned. It looked as if he was going to take a swing at Gina.

"If you ever hit her I will kill you," Lily slowly said. In a very calm voice she added, "I need you to leave."

"I take care of this family!" he snapped.

"Except dad, you don't," Gina said softly, shaking.

Suddenly Gina ran to the basement. She grabbed her father's empty alcohol bottles. She felt nauseous bringing them into the kitchen. Lily looked in shock as Gina put them on the kitchen table. "See? You don't take care of us!"

Ted rose from his chair. He picked it up and flung it against a wall. Lily immediately moved in between Gina and Ted. He tried to find the car keys on the table. Lily grabbed them before he could find them. He scowled at her and left. He slammed the door behind him.

Lily burst into sobs. Gina locked the door after him. Gina hugged her. "Gina, I have a show. I have to go to the theater. I hope you can forgive me for this," Lily choked out.

"It's okay, Mom. You have a show. I will be fine here."

"No, I don't care what the rules are. You just saw your father being violent. You are old enough to see this ballet and understand it. You are going with me. You can watch from the wings," Lily said.

Gina sat in the dressing room with Lily. She watched Lily put up her hair. She did her make up. Her hands shook as she dressed in tights. Then she put on a flesh colored leotard with black lines painted on it. Lily was playing a spider, or some kind of insect.

Gina memorized how her mother tied the ribbons on her pointe shoes. "One day I will tie my own," she thought.

Lily handed Gina a program. "This is what the ballet is about. I play the Novice."

"What's a Novice?" Gina asked.

"A beginner. I am the daughter of the Queen." Lily indicated another dancer in the dressing room. She was affixing jewels around her eyes in lines that swept above her eyebrows. Lily's make-up was simple, with no jewels on her face.

Gina opened a program and read the plot. Lily touched up her make-up.

Gina read to herself, "There is a tribe of female insects. They kill their male partners. The daughter of the Queen, the Novice, is born. Her cocoon is removed. The Novice meets a male in-sect. Following her animal instincts, she stabs him. She cracks his neck until he dies."

Gina whispered to Lily, "You get to pretend to kill a man?"

Lily smiled, "Twice!"

Gina laughed quietly behind the program. She read on, "The tribe celebrates that the Novice has made a kill. The second male insect appears. The two fall in love and mate."

She looked in shock at Lily. "Mom! You mate on stage!?"

"We roll around on the floor a little. It's sort of

a Disney version," Lily answered. She dabbed powder on her cheekbones.

Gina looked back at the program. She read, "The tribe returns. The couple tries to hide, but are discovered. The tribe attacks the male insect. Finally, the Novice is overcome by animal instincts and kills him. Oh, I see. You kill the second one, too."

Gina read, "The Novice is embraced by the Queen. The rest of the tribe salute her."

"Wow," Gina said. She looked in the mirror at Lily. "Mom, I guess I understand the plot. Do you understand all of it?"

"Not well. That's why I made up my own story to go with the plot. The story that I wrote makes more sense to me."

Gina nodded. "Oh, yeah. I remember."

The stage manager appeared. Lily was told, "Places." Gina was allowed to watch from the wings.

Gina whispered, "Merde," to Lily as she waited in the wings. Gina made herself as small as possible in the wing. She could not be in the way of the other dancers. Gina heard the opening strains of Stravinsky's *Concerto in D*. She peeked out onto the stage, making sure she could not be seen by the audience. There were spiderwebs of ropes hanging from the ceiling. A tribe of female insects danced onto the stage.

Gina held her breath as Lily went out with the Queen. The Queen was frightening. She danced expressionless, with an insect's unblinking eyes.

Lily as the Novice, gave questioning looks to the Queen. After her first kill, she swelled with confidence. She danced with passion when she fell in love with the second male insect. With a snap of her head and a look of understanding, she killed him, too.

The ballet finished. The dancers took their bows. The applause was loud and long. It increased when the Queen took her bow. When Lily bowed, cheers broke out. Most of the audience leapt to its feet.

Gina waited for Lily to change. They passed through the lobby and were greeted by Uncle Gene. Gina raced to hug him. He took Lily's dance bag from her.

"Gene! I didn't know you would be here!" Lily smiled.

"I wouldn't miss it. You were magnificent! Let's go for ice cream?" Gene suggested.

"Yes!" Gina replied.

At the ice cream parlor, Gina ordered vanilla with pecans and caramel. Lily had raspberry.

Uncle Gene wanted butter brickle, but they no longer sold it.

"I wonder why they don't have butter brickle?" Gene wondered.

"Because it's icky," Lily replied.

"That's true, Uncle Gene. No one orders butter brickle. Maybe grandmothers," Gina added.

He contented himself with licorice ice cream. Gina raised her eyebrows, but didn't say anything. "Ugh, another yucky flavor," she thought.

"That was a weird story, Lil. I liked it," Gene said.

"It was. It was exciting to dance that part," Lily said.

"You were great, mom."

"I agree! You were great, Lily. I'll walk you two back to your car." Gene rose to leave.

Gina was silent most of the way home. Her mother drove the car. When they reached home, she carefully checked the yard. She made sure Ted was not near the house. They listened at the door. They did not hear sounds inside the house and entered. Lily carefully locked the back door. Gina checked that the front door. All of the windows were locked. "I'll have the locks changed," Lily assured Gina.

Getting ready for bed, Gina called out to Lily,

"Mom, what is it like to play the role of someone who kills two men?"

Lily appeared at Gina's door in a robe. "Tonight, I thoroughly enjoyed it." She kissed Gina and left to go to bed.

Gina thought, "I guess I enjoyed it, too." She snuggled into her bed. The room was hot and smelled of cedar paneling. Her fan did little in the heat. "I wonder what it feels like to have so many people love your performance? Will that ever happen to me?"

She was awakened later. The sound of angry voices came through her open window. In Gina's neighborhood few could afford air conditioning. Often there were power outages and the fans suddenly stopped.

On stifling hot, humid, summer nights young couples in the neighborhood could not sleep. They argued and fought about money, the heat, and too much work. The fights spilled out onto tiny lawns. Sometimes the police came to break things up.

"I hope no one is fighting out on the lawn," Gina thought. She got up and looked out a window. She saw a couple across the street entering their house. "They must have been the voices I heard," she thought.

Gina looked down. The window overlooked the back door of their house. She watched as Ted slit the screen on the door. Then he broke the window on the inner door. He reached in and unlocked the door. She watched as he entered the house.

Gina froze. She heard Lily asking him to leave. Then she heard a scream. Gina raced downstairs. Her mother had fallen to the kitchen floor. Gina saw blood everywhere.

"Gina, call the police!" Lily yelled. She held a towel to her head.

Her whole body shaking, Gina called. She reported the attack. She gave their address in a trembling voice. Ted ran past her out of the house.

"No, he ran away," Gina reported to the dispatcher.

"Gina, Please go change. Get me a coat. I'm afraid to get dressed. I need to keep pressing on the cut." Lily was now sitting up in a kitchen chair.

Gina scrambled into clothes. She grabbed a raincoat for Lily. She returned to the kitchen as the police arrived.

"He shoved me and I fell back. I hit something and cut my head," Lily explained.

A second policeman entered the room. He announced, "They saw him about six blocks away.

We will keep looking for him. An ambulance is on the way for you."

"I would like my daughter to come with me," Lily said. She pointed to Gina. "Once they sew me up I'll call my brother to take us back to his apartment."

"Good plan. Will you press charges?" the officer asked.

Lily began to cry, "Yes, I will."

Gina woke up the next morning in her Uncle Gene's apartment. She rubbed her eyes. She remembered he had come to the hospital and taken them to his place.

Breakfast was grim. Gene had gone out and bought croissants for them. Mrs. Popova came up from her apartment. She set out ptitsa bread and orange juice.

"Your brother, Yevgeny, make coffee. Men only make coffee," she said to Lily.

Her English was heavily accented with Russian. Gina remembered that Mrs. Popova called her uncle, Yevgeny. Mrs. Popova gave Lily some flowers from her garden. She kissed Lily's cheek, and left.

Lily smiled. "That was sweet of her. Gene, thank you for letting us stay. Gina, are you all right?"

"I'm fine, mom. The police and Uncle Gene

came to the rescue. I never want to see dad ever again. Is 'Yevgeny' Russian for Gene?" Gina asked.

"Yes. The locks on your house are being changed this morning," Gene said sipping coffee. "Ted showed up here last night."

"He did?" Lily asked, surprised.

"After you and Gina went to sleep. I saw him in the yard. I called the police. They arrived without lights or sirens. They arrested him quietly," Gene explained.

"Thank you, Gene. I will order bars to be put on the windows this afternoon," Lily added. "We are giving him no more chances."

"And you will call my attorney," Gene reminded Lily.

"Yes. I will call him as soon as he is open on Monday. Gina, I am divorcing your father."

"I know I'm not supposed to say this, mom. I never really liked him," Gina admitted.

Gene looked up. He nodded in agreement.

"Why didn't you say so? I would have left him ages ago," Lily said.

"Thou shalt honor thy father and thy mother? You sent me to Catholic school," Gina said.

"Oh, that. I didn't think you'd actually believe in all that," Lily said.

"Well, I did," Gina laughed. She threw a napkin

at Lily. "Why did you marry him, anyway? Didn't you know he was awful?" Gina asked.

Gene coughed.

Lily looked at her brother. "I know you warned me and I should have listened." Lily paused and drank some orange juice.

"I will tell you one thing," Lily sighed. "I met Ted. He was up all night playing jazz in clubs, sleeping all day. I was at ballet class, rehearsals, and evening performances. We were never to-gether enough to get to know each other very well. But, we had Gina and that is all that matters."

"It is," Gene agreed.

Gina took a bite of croissant. She wondered if things were getting better. She swallowed and thought, "Life will be better. Soon. I will make sure I help mom more."

15

A few days after the summer solstice, Lily woke Gina. She heard Prince singing "*In France, a skinny man died of a big disease with a little name*," on the radio.

"We are going to Loring Park today. I made tee shirts for us. Rainbow tie-dye with *A Generation of Pride* written on them. It's the theme this year."

"It's Pride today?! You've been talking about it for weeks!" Gina exclaimed.

"And we're going with Ben!" Lily told her.

"Your ballet partner? Cool! Why doesn't dad like him? Oh, yeah. Ben is gay. Why can dad be such an idiot about so many things?" Gina asked.

"Fear of the unknown. Deep insecurity. He was abused so he needs to abuse others," Lily replied.

"Mom, remember today is a fun day. Anyway, I've never been to Loring Park." Gina put on her tee shirt.

"This year Pride celebrates the twentieth anniversary of the Stonewall Revolution. Ben can tell you more about that."

"What was the theme last year?" Gina asked. She pulled on shorts.

"Rightfully Proud," Lily replied. She tucked flowers into her hair and some into Gina's.

"Are we meeting Ben there?" Gina asked.

"Yes. And we are taking the bus. You can't park within miles of the park. They are expecting ten thousand people to march and celebrate."

"Are we going to march?" Gina asked. "That would be so great!"

"No, we'll set up at the park and greet the people who marched. Remember sunscreen!"

After a quick bus ride across the city they got out at Loring Park. The park was beautiful and green, with benches, flowers, and many old trees. There was a large pond in the middle.

"Look!" Gina noticed a banner waving. It had STONEWALL REVOLUTION written on it. "Is that what you were talking about, mom?" she asked pointing.

"Yes, police arrested people for being gay in 1969 at the Stonewall bar in New York City."

They heard a man's voice behind them. "Within weeks, the people of the neighborhood organized. They fought for places for gays and lesbians to gather without fear of being arrested."

"Bizi!" Lily turned. She and Ben hugged. "This is my daughter, Gina."

Gina hugged Ben. "I thought your name was Ben?"

"It is, for people who don't know me well. Your mom, Zizi, knows me very well."

"Why do you call mom Zizi?" Gina asked.

"It is in Anishinaabe, my native language. Zizi is short for Zaagaasikwe. It means Shining Light."

They walked along a path. There were crowds of people dressed in rainbow colors. Lily waved at several friends who passed by.

"You speak a native language? Wow," Gina said.

"I am Anishinaabe from Sault Sainte-Marie in Canada. We are the people of the rapid waters," Ben explained.

"What does Bizi mean?" Gina asked.

"It's is short for Bizaan. The elders gave the name to me at birth. It means peace or quiet."

"You talk all the time! I've heard you and mom on the phone. She hardly says anything."

"I think the elders don't always get it right. Yes, Bizi?" Lily laughed.

"Can I have a name?" Gina asked. She tugged on Ben's sleeve.

He replied, "Giniijaanis."

"A name for me! What does it mean?" Gina asked.

"It means My Child. Gini for short."

"It's a lot like Gina," Gina pointed out.

"I can't change the whole language for you." Ben smiled down at her.

"I love it. And we will have fun today at Pride. Mom told me it's beautiful."

"It is. Let's find a table," Lily said.

They found a spot at a picnic table with others enjoying Pride. Lily had packed sandwiches, chips, and cookies. Ben brought sodas and fresh raspberries and blackberries.

"What else do the elders do?" Gina asked. She munched on chips.

"Well, they helped my brother. He was born with too many sensitive powers. They knew his personality couldn't handle it. The elders gathered and prayed. They gave him a special tea to drink. He has been calm ever since," Ben explained.

"I wonder if Mrs. Lemieux has sensitive powers? Mom, do you know?" Gina asked.

Lily explained, "She is a nurse who works with AIDS patients. When they die, she escorts them to the spirit world. Then comes back to our world."

"Ben, does she have sensitive powers?" asked Gina.

"Yes, she does. And we are very lucky to have Mrs. Lemieux. I have been to the funerals of many friend who have died of AIDS," Ben said.

"Look!" Gina pointed. There was a man dressed in a blue tight shirt, tights, a yellow cape, and white boots. The letter "C" was printed on his chest. He wore a white plastic pointed cap on his head.

Ben smiled and said, "It's Captain Condom. He's handing out condoms. The condom has saved many lives from AIDS."

"Do you have a boyfriend, Ben?" Gina asked.

"I am Niizh-manidoowag, a two-spirit. I have both a feminine and a masculine spirit. So, I love both men and women. At the moment, I am single."

"Okay. Why is the celebration at Loring Park?" Gina wondered.

"My Child asks excellent questions! Gays have been beat up or murdered in Loring Park," Ben told her.

"Just for loving each other? That's horrible!"
Gina said.

"It is. There are gay gangs. They patrol the parks to protect gays from getting beat up. I'm in one. I'm a Pink Panther."

"You're amazing, Ben. And you can dance!" Gina said. Ben laughed.

"But, back to brighter things!" Lily suggested.

"Yes, Shining Light," Ben said to Lily.

"How did the parade start?" Gina asked.

"It began as a march in 1972. About fifty of us got together at Loring Park. We decided Loring Park had to be part of the march because so many people had been killed or hurt here," Ben explained.

"You were there?" Gina asked. She reached for a blackberry.

"I was. I was a teenager. It was an exciting day," Ben answered.

Ben continued, "Half of us waited in Loring Park. The other half marched down Nicollet Mall. We thought for sure the marchers would be arrested. The group waiting in the park would come and bail us out of jail."

Lily smiled. "And then the most wonderful thing happened. The police never showed up to arrest them."

"I was one of the marchers on Nicollet Mall. I waved my picket sign and chanted about gay pride. We marched all the way back to Loring Park. We joined our friends waiting for us," Ben smiled.

"And then you had a picnic!" Gina exclaimed.

"Just like we are, My Child," Ben said.

Gina looked around. She saw men walking hand in hand. She saw women hugging, children playing, and families celebrating. People played guitars. Others danced.

"I like this. It is beautiful, mom. We should invite the police to come to this picnic," Gina suggested.

"I imagine there are some off-duty police here. Probably dressed in jeans and tee shirts," Lily said.

"I bet you're right, mom! Who knows?" Gina smiled.

16

One hot, humid day, Lily drove them to visit her cousins. She liked going to see them. Her Aunt Maggie and Uncle Bob were kind and welcoming. Her four cousins were energetic, athletic, and excited to see to Gina. They affectionately called her "our pale cousin from the city."

Her cousins were all older than Gina and in the 4-H Club in their neighborhood. In the past they had showed her their rock and butterfly collections. They knew how to tie knots and make campfires. Gina liked being with her cousins, but she knew she wasn't like them.

Gina looked out from the car as they approached their three-story house. It sat on a hill across from a large, beautiful lake. Her cousins swam in it all summer long. Fourteen year-old Nancy and eleven year-old Jeff came out to meet the car.

"Gina, come on. We're going swimming!" they called.

Gina ran into her cousins' house with them. She changed into her one-piece pink swimsuit. She accepted a towel from her aunt. She walked across the street with her cousins to the house where the Swan family lived. Their backyard ended in the lake. There was a long wooden dock with a rowboat moored to it.

She watched one of the Swan children, Tony, climb into a tire. The tire was attached to a long rope tied to the branch of a very tall tree. Jeff walked a long way back from the lake holding the tire. When he had gone as far away from the lake as the rope would reach, he let go. Tony and the tire sailed out over the lake. Tony jumped from the tire into the water.

After a moment Tony surfaced. He was laughing and swam to shore. "That was fantastic!" he said.

A few more children took turns sailing out over the water and making the jump. Finally, only

Gina had not taken a turn. Nancy said, "Gina, you have jump! It's so fun! It's a blast!"

Gina climbed into the tire. Nancy walked a long way back from the lake holding the tire with Gina in it. She let go. Gina sailed out over the lake. She heard yelling, "Gina! Jump! Let go!"

In that moment, all Gina could think of was failing swimming lessons when she was seven. And about her Uncle Matthew, Lily and Gene's little brother. Matthew had drowned at the age of seven. As soon as Gina turned seven, Lily enrolled her in swimming lessons. For the final lesson each child was asked to jump into the deep end of the swimming pool and swim.

At that final lesson, Gina followed her instructor's directions. She had jumped. She thought of her mother's little brother and had panicked. She had flailed her arms wildly and called to her teacher for help. He reluctantly swam to Gina to help her to the side of the pool. He had told her he was disappointed in her.

She continued sailing out over the lake. She heard her cousins encouraging her. "Gina! Let go! Jump!"

She let go of the rope. She was flung very far out over the water. She hit the surface and fell, deeper and deeper toward the bottom. She finally opened her eyes. Through waving weeds she saw the sun shining far above her.

It was too quiet. She was more frightened than she had been in her swimming lesson. She remembered to kick her legs. She strove to reach the surface of the water. She struggled and struggled, feeling long minutes go by. Nearly frozen in fear, she finally popped her head out of the water. She reached fresh air.

Her cousins were jumping up and down on the shore. They shouted, "Gina, you were great! You are so cool!"

She breathed deeply thinking, "My secret is safe. No one knows I can't swim." She smiled and waved at her cousins.

Gina tread water. Jeff rowed out to her in a rowboat. "Great jump, Gina. We thought you might like a lift back to the dock."

She clambered in gratefully. "That was, oh wow, everything!" she lied. She smiled up at Jeff. "You didn't have to come and get me. I would have been fine swimming to the dock, but thanks."

Gina turned to get a towel. Jeff looked at her back. "Hold still!" he said.

"What?! What is it?" Gina asked.

"A leech. On your back," he said.

Gina screamed, "Get it off! Please! Get it off!"

He successfully pried the slimy creature off of her. He threw it in the water. "There it's over. You're okay now."

Gina felt nauseous seeing the leech in the water, knowing that it had touched her. "Thanks for getting it off."

"No problem! We get them all the time," Jeff said. He rowed toward shore.

Gina thought, "That was horrible, and on top of almost drowning. It still isn't as scary as thinking about performing ballet on stage. That's truly terrifying."

Later after a picnic, Lily and Gina walked to the car. Her Aunt Maggie had put a large bag in Lily's car. It was filled with clothes that her daughters had outgrown. Gina looked through them and sighed. At least her aunt couldn't see how disappointed she was.

Lily glanced over at Gina. "Brown, yellow, and orange," they said together.

"Why couldn't I have had cousins with dark hair, pale skin, and green eyes like me?" Gina asked.

Lily chuckled. "I don't know. Your cousins all have dark eyes and tans. They do look good in those colors. I'm sorry. Did you have fun today?"

Gina thought about nearly drowning, being devoured by a leech, and the gift of clothes she didn't like. She lied carefully, "It was good, mom. I like my cousins. But, I am sunburnt and tired."

"Then it's good we're going home."

<h1 style="text-align:center">17</h1>

The next day at the end of ballet classes, Gina curtsied for Madame as usual. She changed into street clothes, and took the elevator down to first floor. She stepped out of the Arts Center and into a torrent of rain. Lightning flashed every few seconds or so. She ran to the bus stop. She was drenched by the time she reached her stop, although she ran as fast as she could.

Gina climbed aboard her bus. She put her fare in the box. She nodded to the bus driver. He knew that she was always at the stop in the afternoons after summer ballet classes. He kept track of where she got off also, although she never missed her stop.

Lightning continued to flash and thunder to

crack. At each stop sopping wet passengers alighted. Soon there was water running down the aisles. It had collected from dripping passengers and their bags, umbrellas, and jackets.

Gina looked out the window at the lightning. She listened to the cracks of thunder. The storm was so strong, bringing with it sheets of heavy rain. The passengers gasped each time the lightning flashed and thunder cracked. Gina watched intently out the window. She thought, "I know this is crazy, but I want to be out running in this!"

The bus stopped at her corner. She leapt out and started running. The lightning felt exciting to her. Every few moments the sky lit up on her way home. She ran laughing. She sloshed and splashed her way through the puddles all the way to her house.

Key in hand, she reached the door. She unlocked the door. Her mother would be home soon. She found flashlights in a kitchen drawer, knowing soon it would be dark. She set about lighting candles. Lily finally came home. She was drenched from running the few steps from the garage.

"I have a new role to work on!" Lily told Gina breathlessly. She had been rehearsing with her ballet company. She stashed her umbrella in the hallway.

Gina hung up Lily's raincoat. "Great, mom! What is it?"

"I'm the Sylph in *La Sylphide*!" Lily announced.

"A Sylph?" Gina handed Lily a towel.

"She is a forest spirit," Lily explained.

"Good costume?" Gina asked.

"It's a dream," Lily said. She dried her hair.

"What's *La Sylphide* about?" Gina asked.

Lily pulled a book of ballet stories out of her bag. "Let's start with the characters. There is James, a young Scotsman. Effie is James' fiancée. Gurn is James' friend. Gurn is in love with Effie, too. There is a witch named Old Madge. I'm the Sylph, a spirit of the forest.

"Not a big cast," Gina remarked.

"There are a lot of other sylphs and townspeople. Here's the story," Lily said, turning a page.

She read aloud. "James is asleep by the fireside on the morning of his wedding. A Sylph comes in through the window. James is awakened by the kiss of the Sylph. The Sylph flies away through the window. He asks Gurn if Gurn saw the Sylph. Gurn tells James he saw nothing. He reminds James that he is soon to be married."

"So, you can rest a little backstage," Gina noted.

"Yes, it's really tough getting in and out of that window looking like a spirit," Lily said.

She continued, "Effie and James welcome the wedding guests. James thinks only of the Sylph's kiss. He sees a shadow by the hearth and thinks it's the Sylph. He approaches the shadow. James instead finds Old Madge, the witch. Old Madge tells Effie's fortune. Old Madge tells Effie, 'You will not marry James. He loves someone else.'"

"I bet Effie was mad," Gina said. She took the book and turned a page. "Huh, I guess not."

Gina read, "Effie leaves to prepare for the wedding, even though Old Madge told her James loves someone else. The Sylph visits James and tells him she loves him. James tells the Sylph he loves her. Gurn sees this and tells the wedding guests. No one believes Gurn. The wedding festivities begin."

Lily took the book and read, "The Sylph flies away. James chases after her."

"Now Effie is mad," Gina guessed.

"Furious. I almost wanted to play Effie instead, but the Sylph costume is so luscious," Lily sighed.

Lily read more. "Now we are in the forest. Old Madge brews a potion in a cauldron. She pulls a scarf out of it."

"It would be fun to play Madge, too," Gina considered. Is there a drawing of Madge?" She took the book. Madge wore black lace and had long gnarled fingers. "Ooh, she's creepy!"

Gina read, "James finds the Sylph in the forest. The Sylph and her friends dance for James. They show him their beautiful home. He tries to capture the Sylph. She escapes. Meanwhile, Gurn proposes to Effie and she accepts."

Gina looked up. "She sure got over James in a hurry."

Lily laughed, "Next is the best part."

She read, "James finds Old Madge. Madge gives James the magic scarf. She tells James to wrap it around the Sylph. Then he will be able to keep the Sylph forever. The Sylph appears. James wraps the scarf around the Sylph. The scarf causes her wings to fall off. She dies. Her sylph friends help the ghost of the Sylph fly away. The wedding procession of Effie and Gurn passes by. James collapses and dies."

"So, are the Sylph and James united forever as ghosts? Although, the Sylph was kind of a ghost anyway," Gina asked.

"She was kind of a ghost. And we never find out if they are together. We get to make up the ending ourselves. The best kind of ending. We need to resurrect Gabriela," Lily suggested.

"Mom, I was little when we did that. It was fun

pretending to be Gabriela and make up stories. I don't need to be her anymore."

Lily looked at her. "Well, maybe I do."

"I'll open the closet!" Gina said. She ran upstairs and opened the door. Out spilled vests, ties, aprons, tutus, frilly aprons, a fedora, and other colorful pieces of costumes.

Lily and Gina furiously acted out every scene. Gina played the doomed Effie, all of the Sylph friends, and Old Madge. Ken dolls stood in for James and Gurn. After they had taken their last bow, they lay puffing on the floor.

"Thanks for letting me play the Sylph. I needed the practice," said Lily.

"Mom, you'll be wonderful. So light. I believed you were a Sylph the whole way through."

"To bed!" Lily said. She danced the way downstairs to her bedroom.

Gina pulled a pale blue nightgown over her head. "Mom is beautiful. Will I ever be that beautiful? I like playing characters like Old Madge, but I'd like to do Sylph parts, too."

The rainstorm continued. Gina dreamed that her mother became ill. Gina had been chosen to dance the Sylph. There was no time to teach her the part. The costume was a little large for her. She waited in the wings. In the dream Gina protested, "I have never danced on pointe! This is awful!"

Old Madge appeared in Gina's dream. Madge shoved Gina onto the stage. "Be the Sylph! Charm and entrance! Show the world how beautiful you are!"

Gina dreamed she collapsed into a white chiffon heap on the floor of the theater. "I can't," she sobbed. "I can't!"

Old Madge picked her up. She forced Gina onto the stage. The lights blinded her. Gina did not know the steps or what to do. The other dancers looked at her expectantly to begin to dance. Gina dreamed she cried out, "No!" She wrapped her Sylph wings around herself and ran off the other side of the stage.

There was a loud crack of thunder. The wind made tree branches hit the roof. Gina awakened. She clutched her comforter to her. "Performing on stage is going to be horrible!" She rolled over, punched her pillow and tried to sleep.

On the bus on the way downtown she thought, "A dream is a dream. It doesn't mean anything. It means I was asleep. I love ballet."

Gina was into the sixth and final week of summer intensive ballet classes. Gina loved it all, but was especially tired every evening.

"I had a bad dream about ballet because I was overtired," she consoled herself.

During the first class Madame Branitskaya stopped. She turned to Gina and said, "Show self more."

Gina continued, unsure of what to do. She performed the steps Madame had given her again.

"No, no, no, no, no. You cannot go on this way.

Show me who Gina is. Show me girl who loves to dance," Madame insisted.

Gina tried again, this time with even more uncertainty.

"No! When we are through today, go home and think about this. Do not return until you can show me," Madame ordered.

The class was silent. Even the pianist looked at Gina.

"We go on," Madame sighed. She waved her hand. All of the dancers took their places to start again. Gina did not give up, but received no praise from Madame that day.

Gina rode the bus home with a grim look on her face. "Maybe the dream did mean something. Maybe I am supposed to quit. I can't go back until I figure out what it is she wants me to do."

At home she told Lily, "I want to quit ballet. I don't know how to do anything!"

"Of course not. You're there to learn."

"I can't go back. I don't know what Madame wants me to do! Or be!" Gina exclaimed.

"Think about it tonight. Make up your mind in the morning," Lily advised.

Gina awakened early the next morning. She found Lily with a coffee and the newspaper in the living room.

"I sort of figured it out, mom. I can show her the girl who loves ballet by going back today. Even though I am scared. You think that's it?" Gina asked.

"I do," Lily smiled. "I am sure of it."

Madame smiled when she saw Gina enter the studio. After one particularly difficult combination, Madame said loud enough for the class to hear, "Good, Gina. I see you now. Girl who loves ballet."

Gina smiled and sighed with relief. The rest of the day went smoothly. Gina smiled all the way home on the bus. The rest of the week she felt much better.

On the final day, she walked from the bus stop to the arts center. She thought, "Ballet is going great. But, I sure am relieved. I'm not on pointe yet. So, I don't have to be in the in-studio performance. Only girls on pointe will perform today."

Gina happily danced all day. She clapped and cheered for the dancers in the show. Soon she was back on the bus. "I'll miss ballet, but I'm tired!"

There were no ballet classes during August. Gina resumed classes with Lily at home. Lily also did not teach ballet during August. She spent the month repainting the studio and installing new flooring. The rest of the time she spent on paperwork and preparing for the following year's tax season.

Gina was often alone, not minding at all. She had read all of the usual books for a sixth grader, *Fabulous Five, The Diary of Anne Frank, The Outsiders,* and *The Hobbit.* She rode her bike to the library. There she found more popular books for teens. The librarian tried to help her.

"I don't like *Babysitter Club* books, or the *Boxcar Kids,* and teen romance is the worst. They're stupid!" Gina admitted to the librarian.

"I know you study ballet. How about a biography of a famous dancer? We have one about Nureyev and a few about Anna Pavlova." She led Gina to the shelves of biographies. She selected two for her. "I think you might like these."

"I'm sure I will! Thank you." Gina accepted the books and checked them out. At home she climbed up to her favorite branch in the birch tree with the book about Rudolf Nureyev. Gina spent the afternoon traversing Siberia, St. Petersburg, and the world with Rudolf.

"Wow! He was born on a train in Siberia," Gina thought. She looked down to see Lily smiling at her.

"Nureyev?" Lily asked, looking up at the cover.

"A true ballet star. I've only seen him dance on television. He is very special."

"And Nureyev left his country to live outside the Soviet Union! Now he can never see his family in Russia again. He didn't have freedom there. Uncle Gene won't have any trouble coming home, will he?" Gina wondered.

"I don't think so. Your uncle knows how to take care of himself. You know, Nureyev is dying," Lily said softly. "Of AIDS."

"Oh, mom. That is awful," Gina frowned.

Lily sighed, "It is. He is a truly great dancer. Let's go in. We should have dinner and then a ballet class to celebrate Nureyev!"

Getting into bed that night Gina thought about Nureyev and AIDS. "How can there be a disease that punishes people for touching each other?" She eventually fell asleep. The room was hot and smelled of cedar. That was nice.

The next day she woke up early.

"Mom, get up! We're going to the State Fair today! Usually I never have to get you up. Are you okay?" she asked.

"I am. I'll get ready quick," Lily said getting out of bed.

Lily and Gina were meeting Aunt Maggie, Jeff, and Nancy at the entrance of the Great Minnesota

State Fair. There were crowds of people there. Finally Gina spotted them. "There they are!"

"Let's go to the Midway!" Jeff suggested.

"Mom, can I?" Gina asked.

"Yes, we will meet you at the Space Needle," Maggie and Lily said. They gave all of them money for rides.

Gina rode the rollercoaster with her cousins. They went into the funhouse. Gina watched Jeff play a game and win a giant stuffed animal. They ate cotton candy and salt water taffy.

Hot, dusty, and tired, they went to the Space Needle to meet their mothers. They never rode the Space Needle. It was a boring ride. Passengers sat in seats and were taken slowly upward. Then the passengers revolved slowly at the top. It gave a view of the entire fairgrounds. Lily and Maggie were there on a bench waiting for them.

"Let's go see the animals?" Gina asked.

"Sure! Yes! Okay!" everyone answered.

They passed through the Dairy Building on the way. The state fair princesses sat there in refrigerators. People looked at the princesses through glass walls. A man was in the refrigerator with them. He carved their likenesses into statues of butter. Gina and her cousins each had an ice cream cone.

They went to the 4-H building. Gina patiently looked with Jeff and Nancy at butterfly and insect collections. They talked excitedly about Lepidoptera and used other long butterfly names.

Next were the cow barns. Gina loved to look at farm animals. All she ever saw in the city were cats, dogs, birds, and squirrels. "The cows and sheep are so calm," she thought looking over the fence of the enclosure. Some of them wore blue ribbons because they had won contests. The building next door held cages and cages of fluffy rabbits.

Gina's favorite part of the fair was the horse barns. Gina's cousins loved the Clydesdales. They were huge horses that had fluffy fur around their feet. Often the Clydesdales were hitched up and pulled a carriage through the fairgrounds. The Clydesdales were a well-known advertisement for Budweiser beer.

Gina loved the Arabian horses the best. Their stalls were the last in the horse barns. Gina loved their elegant faces and long arched necks. She petted one with large beautiful eyes.

The day ended with foot long hotdogs. Gina said "Good Bye" to her aunt and cousins at the entrance.

"Did you have fun?" Lily asked. She carried a bag of Minnesota grown apples.

"I did, mom. But, school tomorrow! Seventh grade! And I still have eighth grade and all of high school left to go. Can we watch *Ferris Bueller's Day Off*?"

"Because it makes fun of school?" Lily asked.

"Yes!!!" Gina laughed.

19

The next day she found a note from Tim in her locker. She read, "Do you want to go to see *Indiana Jones and the Last Crusade* with me? Write me back, Tim."

"I don't want to be alone with him!" she thought. "What if he asks about the things my dad did?" She crumpled up the note. She put at the far back of her locker.

Classes finished for the day. As students walked out, Sister Aquinas asked Gina to wait a moment.

"How are you, Gina?" Sister asked.

"I'm fine, Sister," Gina politely replied.

Sister paused for a second. Then she asked, "Gina, what is your definition of love?"

Gina answered, "To care about someone else more than yourself."

"No. Love means loving yourself first. Only then can you love anyone else," Sister Aquinas told her.

Gina frowned slightly. "I have never heard of such a thing. Are you asking all the kids this question?"

Sister Aquinas sighed. "No, I am not. And perhaps it was not quite fair of me to ask it of you. You may go. Please give your mother my regards."

"Thanks, Sister. Bye," Gina said. She shyly turned away and walked out of the room. "What was that all about?" she wondered.

Gina walked home alone. "This feels weird," she thought. "Walking alone in the morning is less weird. Sharie and Phil and me were always hurrying so we wouldn't be late. Going home we always walked slowly and messed around."

It was still very hot weather. Gina carried her navy blue sweater. She undid the top button of her white Peter Pan collar. She thought about Phil as she passed by his house. It took her a little out of her way, but she wanted to feel close to Phil again.

"I miss him," she thought. "I miss Sharie, too, but at least I can call her on the phone. Phil was my leprechaun. Probably good I never called him that to his face," she mused. "I don't know if a boy would want to be told they are someone's leprechaun."

Lily looked up as Gina came in the back door. "Did you walk by Phil's house again?"

"I did. There was something wonderful about him. Not like a boyfriend. Just like a good friend. He told me stuff about boys that girls should know."

Lily asked, "Like what?"

"Well, that boys like more than anything to make you laugh. That they are afraid of stuff, just like girls are. That they wonder if they look okay, if their clothes are right, like I do," Gina explained.

"He was a great friend. You never know. You might see him again. You could write letters," Lily suggested.

"He would never write back. He hates writing. It took everything Sharie and I could do to get him through English class last year. Mom, you don't have to rush off to the studio tonight. Let's climb up and sit in the backyard maple tree."

"Why?" Lily asked.

"Because I can see Phil's house if I climb up high enough."

"Okay. Let's do it!" Lily agreed.

Gina climbed up high into the tree. Lily stayed

perched on a lower branch. She hung on more tightly than Gina.

"Gina, I haven't done this since I was a little girl. Plus, I have given birth, you know." Lily finally found a comfortable branch. She swung her feet below her.

Gina, up higher, looked down at her mother. "Mom, you only had me. What would you have done if you had had twelve children? Like those three super Catholic families that live across the street from school? Some of the kids still live in those houses. They are all grown up."

"If I had twelve children we'd have a much bigger tree! I only wanted to have you. I would never want to have twelve children," Lily said.

"Think of washing dishes and doing the laundry. It would be endless!" Gina agreed.

Lily looked up at Gina. "I went to school with kids from each of those families. I wondered how their parents had possibly gotten them ready for school every morning. But, there they were, on time, in uniform. Their teeth had been brushed, hair was combed, homework done."

"That's thirty-six kids in all. And only six parents. Think of all their shoes! No wonder those three houses are so big. Did they all go on to have great lives, growing up with all that love?" Gina asked.

Lily laughed. "No. At least one family didn't. I knew one of the girls from the family that lived in the big yellow house. All fourteen of them would come to church on Sunday. They took up an entire row. They were beautiful, all black-haired, blue-eyed, and freckled. The parents were tall and slender and perfectly dressed."

"What happened?" Gina asked.

"The mother of the family decided she didn't love her husband anymore. She fell in love with one of the nuns from your school. She asked her husband to leave the house. The nun moved in. The girl I went to school with had already moved out. The youngest children still lived there. The younger ones had a hard time. They missed their dad."

"She had twelve children. Then she decided she didn't want to be with her husband? Wow. I feel bad for the dad," Gina commented.

"It was hard on the family. Her husband was devastated. He never got over it." Lily held a leaf between her thumbs. She blew over it until it produced a little whistle.

Gina looked down again. "Did the nun stay a nun? I mean, that's against the rules, right?"

"Yes, she left the church. Once the last of the children were grown, the mom and the nun left. They got their own place. I think the youngest son and his wife live in the big yellow house now," Lily said.

"They do. And they already have five kids. They are all littler than me. I see the grandpa visit, but not the grandma. The grandma is the one who fell in love with the nun?" Gina asked.

Lily nodded. "Maybe the family doesn't want to see her. She broke her husband's heart. I hope someday they let the grandma back into their life."

"Me, too. It's not really like with us and dad, is it? He hurt us so much. On purpose. I don't think the mom fell in love with the nun to be mean. Dad seems like he enjoys being angry," Gina said.

"I wish it could have been different for you, Gina," Lily sighed.

"It wasn't. And there's nothing else to say. I'm going to climb down." Gina held a hand out to Lily.

Lily reached up a hand to Gina. They climbed down the last bit of the tree together.

Gina came in the back door the next day after school. Lily was at the kitchen table. She was looking through the mail.

"Mom, something good happened today," Gina announced.

"What's that?" Lily asked, looking up.

Gina sat down. "Sister Margaret Mary told us in morning announcements that Pope John Paul II hugged a boy with AIDS. The pope was visiting San Francisco. That's so great and loving. Will the pope get AIDS?"

"It's not that easy. Look, we got this in the mail a while ago. I forgot about it. It's a pamphlet from the Surgeon General." Lily handed it to Gina.

Gina saw *Understanding AIDS* on the cover. She

took a look inside. "Oh, AIDS has to be caught through blood. Is AIDS what that dancer in your company had before he died?"

"He did. I haven't wanted to talk about it. It's too sad. His boyfriend is lost," Lily sighed.

"I'm sorry, mom. Don't they have medicine for AIDS?" Gina asked.

"There is one called AZT. It's too expensive for most people who have AIDS. Two more of my friends and one of my old teachers have AIDS now. They can't afford it."

Gina sighed, "That's evil."

Lily looked at her sadly. "I agree. Anyway, let's not think about that right now. It's your birthday!"

Lily sang, "Happy, happy birthday to every girl and boy. Hope this birthday present brings you lots of joy... Mrs. Lemieux brought you a gift while you were at school."

Gina opened it. "Oh, it's wild rice! She and her family must have gone ricing and gathered it for us."

"I'm making chicken and rice for your birthday. I'll put in some wild rice. Mrs. Lemieux sent the rice to bless both you and our home."

The phone rang. Gina answered it. She turned to Lily and said very seriously, "Mom, it's Madame. She wants to talk to you."

Lily took the phone. She said, "Hello, Madame Branitskaya." Lily listened and soon smiled broadly, "Yes, Madame, I will make sure she is there and thank you." Lily replaced the receiver in its cradle.

"What is it?" Gina asked breathlessly. "Something bad?"

Lily hugged her. "No, of course not. Madame would like you to appear with her company in the *Nutcracker Suite.*"

"Mom, no! I can't! I'm too scared!" Gina protested.

"Well, let's talk about this. No one will know it is you. You will be the tiniest mouse. You will wear a mask," Lily explained.

"What if I make a mistake?" Gina asked anxiously.

"Since you will be the tiniest mouse, you will have your own movements. You don't have to match the other mice. No one would ever know if you made a mistake," Lily told her.

Gina breathed in, "Then, I'll do it. But don't expect too much. I'm only a beginner."

Lily hugged her again. "You will be an exquisite littlest mouse. Your uncle is coming for dinner."

Gene arrived and they sat down to dinner. The chicken and wild rice dish was wonderful. Lily's cake was, too. Gina wished and blew out candles. She opened an envelope from her uncle. It was tickets for the three of them to see *Walt Disney World's Peter Pan on Ice*.

"Uncle Gene, thank you!" Gina exclaimed.

"And it's tonight. Open this other one before we leave." He handed her a box.

Gina ripped the paper off a large box. "What is it?"

"A short-wave radio!" he announced.

"What do I do with it, Uncle Gene?" Gina wondered.

"You can listen to the news and other programs from other countries. In Spanish, or French, Italian, any language almost!" he explained.

"But, I don't know any of those languages," Gina said.

"Hearing the sounds of other languages will help you develop an ear for them. Maybe someday you'll want to learn another language," Gene suggested.

"Oh, okay. Thank you. I hope I learn another language someday. I'm going to change for *Peter Pan*!" Gina jumped up from the table and went to her room.

They drove downtown and Gene parked in a

lot. They walked to the ice arena. "I'm glad the play is *Peter Pan*. I love Tinkerbell," Gina said.

"Why?" Gene wondered.

"Because she's adorable and tiny and mad all the time," Gina answered.

"It's true. That's why I like Tinkerbell, too. Women can't really be mad. Men don't like it," Lily wisely added.

"Do you know where she comes from?" asked Uncle Gene.

"No, Uncle Gene. But I think you are going to tell me," Gina replied.

"Sir James Barrie created Peter Pan and Tinkerbell. He was born and educated in Scotland and then moved to London. In London he met the neighbor boys, the Davies. They inspired him to write about a boy who has magical adventures in Neverland.

"James even took care of the Davies boys after their parents died," added Lily.

"That's true. When James was six, his older brother David died in an ice-skating accident. It was the day before David's fourteenth birthday. Their mother never recovered from David's death. James tried to fill David's place. He wore David's clothes and whistled like him," Gene explained.

"Poor James! That's horrible! He tried to become David?" Gina asked.

"In a very sad way. James' mother loved imagining that David was a fourteen year old boy forever. Since David had died, he could never grow up or leave her," Gene continued.

"Gene, let's get to Tinkerbell!" Lily suggested.

"James wrote Tinker Bell as a tinker fairy who fixed pots and kettles. Her voice is the sound of a tinkling bell. Sometimes she is angry, jealous, mean, and curious. At other times she is helpful and kind to Peter," Gene told them.

"How can she sometimes be mean and sometimes kind?" Gina wondered.

"She is so tiny that she can't feel more than one feeling at a time. She can't fit more than one feeling in. So, if she is angry, she only feels anger. She can't fit in compassion for the person she is mad at," Lily explained.

Gene laughed, "Her favorite insult is 'You silly ass!' On stage 'You silly ass' is always represented by four musical notes followed by a growl on the bassoon."

"But, Uncle Gene, what about the pixie dust? That's her best thing. And her costume," Gina asked.

"Wings are always a nice touch," Lily agreed.

"The pixie dust! James Barrie added it to the story. Many children learned how Peter and Tinkerbell flew. They tried to fly from their beds and hurt themselves," Gene said, turning a corner. "Barrie wrote that no one could fly without Tinkerbell's pixie dust. It was impossible to get pixie dust. So, children stopped jumping out of their beds."

"Here we are." Lily indicated a line of children and adults stretching to the entrance of the arena.

They showed tickets. Gene led their way through the swarms of people juggling popcorn and candy. Their seats were in the first row in the center on one of the long sides of the oval arena.

In the row behind them, they heard a man say to his wife, "Wow. Great seats. If only this was a hockey game."

Gina giggled. The lights went down. In a cheerful glow, skaters came onto the ice that turned into a party in London. Women wore Victorian dresses with large sleeves and bonnets. The men wore cutaway suits and tall hats. The Darling parents put the young boys, John and Michael Darling and their older sister, Wendy, to bed during the party.

That night, the children were visited in the nursery by Peter Pan. He taught them to fly with the help of Tinker Bell and her pixie dust. The skater playing Peter Pan was playful, and full of youthful energy.

"Tinkerbell is the best! She looks like she's flying, even though she's on skates!" Gina whispered to Lily.

Peter took the children with him to the island of Neverland. A pirate ship appeared on the ice. The ship's captain, Hook, plotted to hurt Peter Pan. Peter had cut off Hook's hand. Gina thought that the Captain Hook skater was wonderful, too. He was old, frightening, and obsessed with power.

Tinker Bell was very jealous of Peter's attention to Wendy. In a rage, she lied to Peter's friends, the Lost Boys. Tinkerbell lied that Peter wanted them to shoot Wendy. Peter found out about the lie and ordered the Lost Boys to never hurt Wendy. He sent Tinkerbell away.

Peter took Wendy to see the mermaids. Tinkerbell disobeyed Peter and came along. She ordered the mischievous mermaids to torment Wendy.

"That was my favorite part, mom. Wendy is such a downer."

"Mine, too," Lily agreed.

Wendy and her brothers invited Peter to return to London and live with them. Peter refused. He did not want to grow up. The pirates planted a bomb to kill Peter. Tinker Bell snatched the bomb as it exploded.

Gina watched breathlessly as Peter rescued Tinker Bell from the rubble. Captain Hook fought Peter. Peter sent a crocodile after Hook. Hook ran away, with the crocodile chasing him. Tinker Bell sprinkled pixie dust. Peter flew Hook's ship to London to return the children.

Gina loved watching the pirate ship fly. The Darling children and Peter waved at the audience. Somehow Tinkerbell flitted around the ship and above the ice.

In the next scene the Darling parents checked on their sleeping children. The parents looked out the window of the children's bedroom. They saw a pirate ship in the clouds. It quickly vanished into the stars.

The crowd clapped long and loudly. Gina, Lily, and Gene made their way to the lobby.

"I'm not sure how they made a pirate ship on ice, but it was beautiful. And it flew! Thank you, Uncle Gene."

They swerved around chattering children and their parents. Gene led them out onto the street. It had rained. Yellow, orange, and red leaves stuck to the pavement. They made their way to the corner to cross.

Gene commented. "It's interesting that Peter Pan is a threat to Hook. Peter brings hope. Hope strikes fear into the greedy, controlling Hook. Peter's courage and bravery make him stronger than Hook. Gina, what do you think?"

Gina gazed up at the streetlights. A fine mist swirled around them. "What, Uncle Gene?" she asked. She was still under the spell of the beautiful play.

"Maybe not just now, Gene," Lily whispered. They continued through the streets of downtown.

21

Gina arrived at school. She opened her locker. "Another note from Tim! I like him. But, he's not like Phil and Sharie. They were fun. All he talks about is baseball."

She remembered Tinkerbell. "Tinkerbell wouldn't want a boyfriend!" It had been weeks since she saw Peter Pan.

"Uncle Gene doesn't have a girlfriend and mom is alone. I don't want a boyfriend. Tinkerbell wouldn't want a boy bothering her all the time! Besides, Tim knows about my dad. I'm always afraid he'll ask me about him."

She quickly scribbled a note to Tim. "I don't want to go with you to see *Indiana Jones*. I don't want a boyfriend. I'm sorry, Gina"

The bell rang. The hallway cleared. Gina slipped the note into his locker. At lunch she watched as he read it. She went over to his table. Tim looked up. Gina said, "I'm sorry. Too much baseball."

He nodded blushing. After school Gina saw him walking with a friendly, sporty girl, Katelyn. They were laughing and talking excitedly about Minnesota Twins baseball. "Perfect!" Gina smiled.

At home Gina opened a letter from her uncle. "Uncle Gene is back in Russia. I hope he is okay," she thought.

She looked at the date on the letter. "He wrote this before he came to see us. Russian mail is so slow," she thought.

August 19, 1989

Dear Gina,

A wonderful thing happened yesterday! I went to a picnic. It was on the border between Austria and Hungary. It was called the Pan-European Picnic.

Russia controls Hungary and East Germany. There is a border fence and wall that East Germans may not cross. Russia does not allow people to cross from East Germany, into Austria. Austria is not under control of Russia. Anyone who tries to cross into Aus-

tria can be imprisoned or shot. It's very complicated. I can't explain all of it.

"No kidding, Uncle Gene!" Gina read further.

The emblem of this picnic was a pigeon breaking through a barbed wire fence. The Austrians invited Hungarians and East Germans. The invitations had 'Break It and Take It' printed on them. People were invited to destroy parts of the border fence and take it away!

We thought a lot of Hungarians and Austrians would come to the picnic. They hate the laws and rules the Russians make them follow. No one expected the East Germans to come.

The plan was to allow only Hungarians through the border gate. I spotted a crowd of people on the Hungarian side. They were walking toward the old gate. They were East Germans! They were carrying everything they owned.

I heard shouts from the Austrian side of the border. Many families had been torn apart when Russia took over. People on the Austrian side called out to the East Germans. East Germans crossing into Austria called back. Their relatives were waiting for them on the other side!

Over six hundred East Germans overran the old wooden gate. The guards let them into Austria! The East Germans were given money. They are staying and making Austria their home. Everyone feasted and sang and danced.

I talked with the Hungarian Prime Minister. He told me that the Russians did not order anyone to be shot or put in prison. The East Germans who came through the gate are free!

Love you!

Uncle Gene

Gina thought "Wow. That was cool. Uncle Gene cares about this freedom stuff. He's a good guy."

"Mom, I'm going up to my room to do homework," she said to Lily. She walked through the living room.

Lily put three cookies on the top of Gina's head. "Balance walking up the stairs with those on your head. It will increase your concentration."

Once alone in her room, she ate the cookies. She stood resolutely in front of the full length mirror. She wasn't going to do homework. "I am going to conquer pirouettes!" she said.

Once again she pictured a string attached to the top of her head. She imagined the string being pulled to the ceiling. She prepared to do a pirouette from fourth position. She knew that the pirouette must be in retire'. Retire' meant putting her right pinky toe under the front of her left knee. Her knee must point sideways.

She must be on full demi-pointe, on tip toe. She should finish the pirouette in exactly this same position. Then she had to gracefully place her right foot into fifth position.

"How can pirouettes be simple and complicated at the same time?" she grumbled under her breath. She turned three quarters of the way round. She ended up stuck there. Her right pinky toe was nowhere near her left knee.

"Okay, I'll try the other way. I will imagine I am screwing myself into the ground as I turn." This was even worse. She lost her balance, slipped, and fell to the floor. "How am I ever going to do these on stage one day? I'm not even in pointe shoes and I'm falling over!"

In the kitchen Lily heard a muffled bump. She glanced at the kitchen ceiling. "Oh, I hope she masters those pirouettes soon. Her knees are covered with bruises," Lily wished. She tossed a salad.

Gina came down for dinner. "How was the homework?" Lily asked. She handed Gina a bowl.

"Oh, fine. I'll need some help with math later, though," she answered casually. She sat down frowning slightly. "I need help with things that rotate 360 degrees."

"The imaginary string pulling you up into the ceiling didn't help?" Lily asked.

"No, and the imaginary screwing myself into the ground didn't either."

"We'll work on pirouettes, then. Much more important than homework," Lily nodded. She sat down at the table.

After dinner they went into the living room. They made extra space to practice pirouettes. Gina took out her notebook and showed it to Lily.

"What is this?" Lily asked.

Gina pointed to a handwritten page. "I make notes of what Madame tells me to do after each ballet lesson."

Lily hugged her. "That is exactly the right thing to do." Lily quickly read through them.

roll shoulders back, shoulder blades flat
   push small of back forward
   lift inner thighs, turn out top of thigh
   lift torso up and forward, lengthen waist
   don't let elbows face floor in second
   really look when you look, don't pretend
   weight on ball of foot, ready to releve'
   think of leg and side of body as one whole leg
   in releve' - lift hips, not heels

transfer weight as you releve' to proper leg
leg directly to the side in retire'
pretend there are a ballons in your armpits
imagine a ball in front of you and that you are
wrapping your arms around it
don't bow head during pirouette

Gina looked at her desperately. "And that's only all the stuff you have to do before you even begin the pirouette!"

"Yes, it is a lot. But, it all must be done." Lily smiled. She looked at the notes again. "I remember Madame telling me these things."

"How do you remember to do all of them at the same time?!"

Lily put the notebook on the floor. "It will become easier, I promise. Your muscles and body will begin to remember for you. It will become automatic. Remember learning to ride a bike? At first it was difficult, but you never have to think about how to do it now. Do you?"

"No. Like learning to read, too. All right, let's get started," Gina said. She stepped into fourth position. Her arms were in preparation.

"Wait! Gina, I have something that will help." After a moment, Lily returned from her bedroom.

She had what looked like a wooden doll in her hand.

"What is that?" Gina asked.

"It's an armature. I used it when I took a drawing class years ago. When you can't afford to take drawing classes with live models you use it. It bends and poses everywhere. Look." Lily positioned the body. She made it into the shape of a perfectly executed pirouette.

"Okay, I see that," Gina said.

Lily bent the armature slightly backward in space. "This is how your body looks when you are doing a pirouette. You fall backwards out of the pirouette. Your body is too busy falling back to complete the full turn."

"I see it! But, how do I fix it?" Gina asked.

"Squeeze your stomach muscles together extra hard. Don't let your upper body fall back. Now, you do," Lily instructed.

"That's what Madame says!" Gina focused and squeezed her stomach muscles together. She turned around one and a half times. "It works!"

Gina made the armature bow to Lily. "Thanks, mom."

"Math?"

"Oh, all right. I'll get my notebook. I only have two problems left," Gina said.

Lily sat down with Gina at the kitchen table. She showed Gina how to do the first problem. "See?"

"Yes," Gina said. She completed the second problem. "Done!"

"You're going to love studying Physics," Lily told her. "Gravity, force, mass, it's what ballet is all about."

"Physics doesn't sound like something I will love. I'm going to go work on pirouettes some more," Gina said.

"And then to bed. Don't stay up to late," Lily said. She headed off to her bedroom.

"No, I won't," Gina said. She stepped into fourth position and prepared her arms. She tried five more pirouettes. "Some were better," she thought.

"Gina, go to bed!"

"Night, mom!" Gina jumped into bed. "Maybe I'll dream I can do pirouettes," she wondered and turned out the light.

22

Gina never knew where to stand, or sit, or to be, except when she was dancing. All uncertainty fell away and she felt grace. She became grace and was not of this world. She belonged to something far greater. Gina did not know how ballet would take over her life in lovely ways.

That night she waited at the bus stop after dance class. Gina breathed in fresh cold air. Snowflakes were gently falling. She could feel them on her face. They melted away quickly on her cheeks. She was still warm from dancing.

The store windows were decorated for Christmas. The major department store's theme this year was Charles Dickens' *A Christmas Carol.* The displays sparkled. There was a moving mechanical

Scrooge, Belle, and the Ghosts. She had a glimpse of Fezziwig's home draped in holly and ivy for Christmas.

Mrs. Adams appeared, after finishing work in the department store. "Gina, dear, you look so happy. It is a joy to see." She put an arm around Gina's shoulder. Soon her bus pulled up. Gina smiled up at her. "Mrs. Adams, have a beautiful night!"

"I will, Gina. Tell your mother I said, 'Hello.'"

Gina waved. She smiled at Mrs. Adams. The bus moved away from the curb and into traffic. Gina glanced up at the glowing circles from the streetlights. She saw snowflakes dancing to the ground.

Once inside the house, she accepted a cup of cocoa from Lily. Gina told her how she felt. "I feel like laughing and crying and singing and dancing all at the same time. What is it?"

"It's joy, Gina. You will feel it again and again," Lily reassured her.

"Why does ballet make joy?" Gina asked.

"Because the body and spirit tell the truth. The mind makes up lies to protect us. The mind tells us stories. The mind tells us that we are heroes, or princesses, or demons. Ballet reveals the joy and the true person inside us."

Gina pulled on a nightgown. She asked, "Dancing is the most wonderful thing in the world. Does ballet take away all my problems?"

"Mmm... For now," Lily said.

"How do you know stuff like this?" Gina asked.

"Years ago I took a Noh dance class. It's a form of Japanese theatre. A master came from Japan to teach one class. I was lucky enough to be chosen to take it. We worked for five hours. All we learned how to do was walk and flutter a fan. I felt like I was innocent and graceful for five hours. My body felt like it knew everything I would ever need to know," Lily explained.

"Mom, I don't know what you are talking about."

"You will. I forgot to ask! How was rehearsal last Saturday? Your *Nutcracker* performances are coming right up."

Gina paused for a moment. "Well, it's different being there all day on Saturdays. Madame marked the floor with tape in the studio. She marked a space exactly the same size as the floor of the theatre."

"Oh, yes. I remember. She sets the entire ballet in the studio, while the sets are being made. Then she transfers the dancers into the theater when the stage is ready," Lily said.

"I've seen all of the roles rehearsed. I love the war between the Nutcracker and the Rat King. It's the best music," Gina commented.

"Have you figured out why the *Waltz of the Snowflakes* is so long?" Lily asked.

"Yes! It's thirteen minutes so the dancers from Drosselmeyer's party can change costumes for everything after *Waltz of the Snowflakes*. Last Saturday we finally moved into the theatre. It was awful! In my mouse dance I put my wrong arm up! Madame laughed. She said that is what you are supposed to do in rehearsal. Mess up. Isn't she great?" Gina smiled.

"I remember that about her, too," Lily nodded.

"The only bad thing is I sneeze in the theater. The orchestra has even started to pause while I sneeze. Then the crew laughs. The other girls make fun of me," Gina admitted.

"They do?"

"They call me Dust Bunny. It's not mean, though. They smile when they say it," Gina explained.

Lily looked at her. "I will make an appointment with an allergist for you."

"What will an allergist do?" Gina wondered.

"Help you breathe better and sneeze less."

"Okay."

Lily looked at her. "You're allergic to the theater."

Gina nodded, sneezing.

"Bless you. I'll make an appointment for an allergist, pronto."

"Aaaachooo! Make it quick!" Gina said, sneezing again.

23

That night after dinner, Lily suggested, "Let's put up the tree tonight."

"It isn't even Thanksgiving yet. Why so early?" Gina asked.

"I think we need cheer early this year. I'm going upstairs to get the stuff," Lily replied.

Gina followed her. "What are we doing for Thanksgiving? I wish Uncle Gene was still here."

"So do I. I think Aunt Maggie and Uncle Bob will invite us as usual. It will be nice," Lily said. She took one end of a fake Christmas tree out of the closet. Gina helped her drag it to the landing.

"Yes, I like my cousins. They are so good at sports. I'm not. I suppose they don't know how to dance," Gina said. She lifted the tree from the other end. She had to keep stopping to scratch her back.

"It was okay going to see Dr. Halverson today. He gave me a needle prick on my back of everything in the world I might be allergic to. I'm definitely allergic to the stuff he gave me!" Gina said. She rubbed her back against the wall.

"I'll put calamine lotion on it," Lily offered.

They carried the tree downstairs. They put it in the corner of the living room. Gina plugged in the lights. "They all work! You're right, mom. This does look cheerier."

Lily went off to get the calamine lotion. She applied it to Gina's back. Gina stopped scratching. "Thanks, mom. Much better."

They gently put the ornaments in place. The tree sparkled and glittered. "Why do we have so many ballerina ornaments?" Gina asked. She fluffed the tutu of one.

"My students at the studio give them to me," Lily replied.

"Every year?"

Lily nodded, "Every year."

They had ballet class that night. The Christmas tree watched them. They didn't have quite as much room for jumping. They did leaps half in the living room, half in the kitchen.

That night Gina dreamed she was dancing the Sugarplum Fairy role. Halfway through the dream, she switched to dancing the Rat King. She was all dressed in black. She had long sharp nails and black pointe shoes. "Way more fun," she thought. She turned over in her sleep.

In the middle of the night the phone rang. Gina froze. "What if it's dad?"

She ran downstairs. Lily was sitting at the kitchen table. "Gina, quick! Turn on the short-wave radio! The Berlin Wall is coming down!"

"Gene, where are you?" Lily asked her brother.

"At the Berlin Wall! I made it just in time to see it come down! I'm in a phone booth," Gene replied.

"How did it happen?" Gina picked up the phone in the bedroom. She listened, too. She cradled the radio in her lap.

Gene explained, "There was a world press conference on East German T.V. at four o'clock today. An East German leader made a mistake. The best mistake ever! He told the world that East Germans were free to leave East Germany. Then all of the journalists asked, 'When, when, when?' The leader said that it was effective immediately."

"Isn't that good? What was the mistake?" Lily asked.

"He forgot to say that East Germans had to

apply for passports before they could leave. And he forgot to say that no one could apply for passports until tomorrow! East Germans called each other. They decided to leave. By ten o'clock tonight, thousands were here at the Wall. The border guards couldn't control the crowds. They started letting people through."

"What is 'vahnzin'? I hear people yelling it?" Lily asked.

"It's the German word, wahnsinn. It means madness!" Gene yelled into the phone. "Everyone is crying and screaming. They are happy to be free. They will be with their families again," he said. "I'm out of coins for the phone. Good Night!"

Lily turned on the television. They watched Germans laugh and cry. People hugged and danced on the Wall. They cut off pieces of the Wall to take home.

Gina turned on the short-wave radio. They listened all night. Every station in the world reported that the Berlin Wall came down. Gina and Lily listened to English, Spanish, Italian, German, and French. They heard many, many languages that they did not recognize.

24

———————

Gina woke up the next morning. She had a cough and a fever. "Back to bed," Lily said. She shook down the thermometer. "It's probably the flu. You'll be better in a day or two."

Gina stayed home from school and ballet lessons. She didn't get better. She rested for three days. She continued to make the mercury rise in the thermometer to one hundred and two degrees.

"I made an appointment with the doctor. The fever should be down by now," Lily said. She changed Gina's bed.

Gina climbed back in. "Okay."

The next day Gina had a chest x-ray. Doctor Wolter determined that Gina had bronchial pneumonia. "Does anyone else at school have this?" he asked. He scribbled out a prescription.

"No. But Amanda in ballet class had a cough. She's been out for a while. She stands next to me at barre. Maybe she has it," Gina answered.

"No doubt. Have this antibiotic prescription filled. Start taking them today. We'll talk in a week. No school or dance class."

"What about *The Nutcracker*?! I have rehearsals!" Gina exclaimed.

"Gina, you have pneumonia. This is a serious illness. I delivered you. I don't want to lose you," he smiled. He put a hand on her shoulder. They rose to leave.

By the time Gina and Lily reached home, Gina was exhausted. She fell asleep on the sofa in front of the Christmas tree.

Lily called Madame. She told her that Gina was too sick to be in the Nutcracker this year. Gina stayed home from school, ballet lessons, and rehearsals. Doctor Wolter would call once a week to check on her. The only thing she could do was rest.

Gina woke up. She went into the kitchen. Lily was writing a letter to school. Gina read it.

·   ·   ·

To Whom It May Concern,

Please excuse the absence of my daughter from her regularly appointed rounds as a student at Our Lady of Victory. The reason for her absence is a congenital thing. She is lazy, and does not like to go to school.

I know that her absence causes a traumatic experience for the other students. I am sure that you have realized this. If you intend to keep your school open you must understand that you can't possibly do it without Gina. Hang in there, pal. She will be back!

With Compassion!

Lily Shostek

"Mom! You can't send this!" Gina protested.

"Why not?" Lily laughed.

"They'll think you're crazy! And I'm not lazy," Gina said.

Lily raised an eyebrow and looked at Gina.

Gina smiled. "Okay. I suppose they know by now that you are a little crazy. You might as well send it," Gina said.

They clinked cocoa cups. Soon Gina was back off to bed.

Gina contented herself with watching videos of *The Nutcracker.* Lily rented them for Gina at the video store. Then she ranked them.

Gina began with *The Nutcracker Movie* from 1973. She didn't like it. She thought, "That was a cartoon, not a ballet at all. The three-headed Mouse King was okay."

After that came the best one, *The Nutcracker.* It starred Mikhail Baryshnikov and Gelsey Kirkland. "She is the prettiest ballerina I have ever seen," thought Gina. She watched from the depths of her blankets.

She felt sad. No Pepe, her mother at the studio all day long and in the evenings at rehearsals or teaching ballet. Every day Gina took her medicines. She did the homework that students dropped off for her. She read.

She stared out the window. The trees were heavy with snow and ice. It was bitterly cold, minus ten, and even twenty degrees some nights. Lily did her best to cheer her up every day. She encouraged Gina to rest. Once when her mother was gone, Gina tried to practice ballet at their ballet barre. She had to give up, coughing and fatigued.

A few days later, she looked at the cover of the box for *The Nutcracker Fantasy.* She decided to skip it. "Another cartoon. Not even a ballet."

She sighed and turned on *Nutcracker: The Motion Picture.* "This one looks interesting," she thought. This one was a real ballet. It opened with Clara. She was dreaming of dancing with a prince. In Clara's dream, her brother, Fritz, lets loose a giant rat. The rat bites Clara's hand. Clara turns ugly. She wakes up from the dream in terror.

Gina thought, "I'd be scared. Her brother is evil. And that rat has seven heads."

She watched Godfather Drosselmeyer give Clara a nutcracker. The nutcracker turned into a prince. Clara and the prince performed a beautiful pas de deux. Then Clara and her Prince fell out of the sky. Before they hit the ground, the Prince turned back into a nutcracker. Clara awakened from the dream.

"Weird ending though," she thought. "And Godfather Drosselmeyer was so creepy. The way he looked at Clara. Yuk."

She heard the mail come through the slot. She got up from the sofa to retrieve the mail. She opened an invitation to Thanksgiving dinner from her aunt and uncle. "I don't think we will be able to go to that this year." She picked up a letter. "Oh good. A letter from Uncle Gene."

November 15, 1989

Dear Gina,

I read about how cold it is in Minneapolis -10 to -20 outside! I hope you are keeping warm.

Did you read this in the news? The Olympic gymnast, Nadia Comaneci, arrived in New York City. She ask for political asylum. It was granted! Her country, Romania, is not a free country. Nadia won gold medals in the 1976 and 1980 Olympics in gymnastics.

Gina looked out the window. "I hope Uncle Gene realizes I have no idea what political asylum is. I guess it means that Nadia can live in the U.S." she thought.

And Russian President Gorbachev met with Pope John Paul the Second! The world is starting to change, Gina! I hope things will become more free for people in Communist countries. Religion is forbidden in Russia.

Gina wondered, "Religion is not allowed? No Christmas? No Easter?"

What you would like for Christmas? I imagine not a Black Watch plaid jumper, or a white blouse with a Peter Pan collar.

Love, Uncle Gene

Gina looked at the last stack of homework and

letters. Students from school had dropped them off. Gina opened one of the letters.

Dear Gina,

We are writing this letter for English. I hope that you're having fun. I bet that you don't know who I am. I am a boy. I wish that you would come back to school so that I can see you again. Do you know what we did in school this last week? We finished our spelling lesson. We beat the other room with our scores.

I wish I was home as long as you were. Are you coming back Monday? I hope so. What are you doing? Just sitting in bed watching TV? If something is funny, I bet it's hard to laugh at it.

Once in English class a bee flew in the room. Instead of paying attention to studying, we paid attention to the bee. When it flew by Wayne he jumped out of his seat. Some girls screamed. Then Sister said, "Why be afraid of a tiny insect?" We still paid attention to the bee. Sister killed it. The fun ended. See you Monday if you come back.

Sincerely,

Your Mystery Friend

P.S. I wonder where that bee came from in the middle of winter?

· · ·

Gina turned the letter over. She examined the envelope. She thought, "I give up. I don't know who wrote it. I bet it was a girl, messing around. I will write to Uncle Gene."

The Coldest Day Ever, 1989
  Dear Uncle Gene,

I am still sick. At least it's winter break. I don't have to do any more boring homework. It's hardly light at all during the day. And it's really, really cold weather! How did you know about it?

Even if I wasn't sick, I probably couldn't go outside. I can't go to ballet class. I can't be in the Nutcracker. All I do is read and watch T.V.

Not much snow. Mom says it's too cold to snow. I remember when I was little. Snow piled up on the boulevards. It was so high, I couldn't see the streets over the snow banks. It was like walking in a tunnel. The trees are bare and black. Well, the pine trees are green. They smell so good.

Thank you for writing to me.
Love, Gina

25

———————

Gina and Lily went to Midnight Mass on Christmas Eve. Gina was feeling better and stronger. They drove on the icy streets to the magnificent Cathedral of St. Paul.

Lily asked Gina, "Do you mind that we don't go to mass on Sundays? I am so tired from working all week, evenings, and all day Saturday. I never think of it."

Gina smiled, "Mom, I go to the most old-fashioned Catholic school in the world. We go to mass every single morning. I have enough masses built up for the rest of my life. I think it's okay."

Lily turned in to the church parking lot. "I've always wondered. Why did you send me to Our

Lady of Victory anyway? Public school is free," Gina asked.

Lily answered, "I went to Catholic school at the Cathedral. And I love the sculpture of Mary on the third floor landing. I always used to touch her toe as I went by."

They walked toward the church. They were surrounded by other families, all dressed for church. The air was cold and crisp. Everyone's boots and shoes crunched in the snow.

"Like the statue at Our Lady of Victory? We have one on second floor. I touch Mary's toe every day, too!" Gina said.

They looked up at the rounded domes and arches of the beautiful Cathedral. It was based on French Beaux Arts architecture.

"Emmanuel Louis Masqueray designed it," Lily told Gina. "He was born in France and studied architecture in Paris. He designed our cathedral to look like a French cathedral. Someday you will see the cathedrals in Paris that inspired him."

"You think I will? How come you never told me this about the Cathedral before?" Gina asked.

"I never told you about the architecture before because I thought you would be bored. You will travel! Maybe with me." Lily held her hand. They crossed the street on the side of the Cathedral.

"I'm not bored! I'm not dad, you know," Gina stated.

"I know. You haven't mentioned him since that horrible night. Are you all right?" Lily asked.

"I'm fine. You have asked me if I am okay every five minutes. It's been months since we saw him. It's okay, mom."

Lily squeezed her hand. They used the small side door.

"It feels like we are part of a family to go in the side door. I'm glad you like going in this little door, Gina. When I climb all those steps at the front of the church, I feel like a visitor."

Gina loved looking up into the dome of the magnificent building. The stained glass windows looked beautiful with candles and lights. The altar was decorated with red and white poinsettias and freshly cut pine boughs. She loved the echo of people's voices saying prayers. She loved hearing the soloists and the organ music from the balcony.

Lily drove them home after mass. Gina could still smell the scent of pine long after they left the church.

"I love the poinsettias, but the pine boughs are the most beautiful," Lily remarked.

"Yes, and they don't make me sneeze!" said Gina.

After she and Lily had gone to bed, Gina read all of the chapters of her favorite books that happened at Christmas. She read the chapters in *Little Women* about how Meg, Jo, Beth, and Amy celebrated Christmas with their mother and Laurie. She checked in on Laura, Pa, and Ma in *Little House on the Prairie*.

Lastly she read the Christmas chapters from each of Maud Hart Lovelace's books. She imagined that she was Betsy, Tacy, or Tib enjoying Christmas with their families. She fell asleep dreaming of other families' Christmases. Gina dreamed of Christmas angels, golden trumpets, and beautifully wrapped Christmas presents.

Gina and Lily made cookies on Christmas day. Lily had no other time to do it. And it helped cover up how little time was needed to open gifts. Ted had sent nothing to Gina, or to Lily.

Her Uncle Gene sent leotards, legwarmers, and a pink dance sweater all made by the Capezio company. Gina knew that Lily had picked out the items and Gene paid for them. She felt warm and thankful to both of them. He thoughtfully included money for tuition. There was a gift certificate for ballet slippers that Gina would need to try on at the Grand Jete' dancewear store.

Lily opened a package with her name on it.

"Mom, I didn't give that to you. Who is it from?"

Lily took off the top. She dabbed *Joy* perfume on her temples and wrists. "Me," she answered.

"You can do that?" Gina asked incredulously.

Lily leaned over and put some on Gina. "Yes, you most definitely can."

Lily touched the softness of Gina's leg warmers and folded them. "How are the other girls in your class? You haven't mentioned them much since you started dancing downtown. I guess I wasn't worried. You seem to love ballet with Madame."

"I do! I don't know. The girls are okay. They really aren't like me. They're really mean to each other. I think because you are a dancer in a company and know Madame they stay away from me. I just avoid them."

Lily sighed, relieved. "Oh, good. Keep ignoring them. It will only get worse as you become more beautiful."

"Really?"

"You can count on it. Should we go see your grandparents?" Lily suggested.

"Yes. I'll get ready."

Lily drove them through the snowy streets to the senior home where her parents lived. It was time for the Christmas lunch for the residents.

They were in the dining room with all of the other residents.

"Mom, you look beautiful!" Lily said, hugging her mother. She looked much like Lily. She had chosen a deep green dress and shawl for the Christmas party. She smiled and hugged Gina. Lily's father had also dressed for the occasion, in a deep grey suit.

Gina wore her favorite red velvet Christmas dress. Lily had on a black sweater and skirt with red piping. They sat down together and enjoyed a festive lunch. They couldn't talk very much. Lily's parents couldn't hear over the Christmas music and all of the other families and residents talking.

It didn't matter. The room was warm and the decorations sparkled. The chef had outdone himself with turkey, ham, vegetables, and many desserts. A harpist had been hired to play during dessert. A Santa Claus came to each table. He presented each lady who lived there with red roses. Each man received a cheese, bread, and sausage basket. Those who lived alone were given both.

After lunch Lily looked carefully at her mother. She asked, "Mom, are you tired?"

Lily's father looked at his wife and nodded. "I think we should go up to our place. This has been a lot of excitement for one afternoon."

"Lily and Gina, Merry Christmas! Thank you for coming to see us," Lily's parents said together.

They all rode the elevator up to the apartment. Lily made sure they were comfortable on their sofa. Gina noticed her grandparents were holding hands. "Good Bye!" she and Gina said. They softly shut the door.

"They seem good, mom," Gina said.

"They do! How about *A Charlie Brown Christmas*?" Lily suggested.

"Yes!"

Lily drove quickly home. Gina put cookies and cocoa on the coffee table. Both of them wrapped up in lambswool tartan blankets on the sofa. Lily put a tape into the player and turned on the television. She settled next to Gina and *A Charlie Brown Christmas* began.

26

Going back to school in January was always tough. This year it was even more difficult. The weather was cold. Snow was piled up everywhere. The skies were grey. Gina had missed so much school she had trouble getting back into a routine. This morning was even worse.

In home room class, Sister Agnes brought in the Lost and Found box from the hall. She called Brian up to the front of the room. His family had little money, Gina knew. He lived in her neighborhood.

Sister selected mittens, a scarf, and a cap from the box. Sister presented them to Brian. She even put the cap on his head. Gina watched in horror.

Sister then directed, "Brian, please thank the

class for the scarf, cap, and mittens. If they hadn't left them behind, they would not be yours."

Brian's face was red and his head was bowed. He mumbled quietly, "Thanks." Taking the cap off, he hurried back to his seat.

Gina raised her hand. Sister looked at her and asked curtly, "Yes. What?"

Gina looked at Brian in anguish. "I think you are hurting Brian." Gina began to cry.

"Gina, please leave and sit in the hall." After a few minutes Sister came out to Gina and waved her back to her seat. "That's it?" Gina thought.

When Sister's back was turned, Brian leaned over to Gina. He whispered, "Thanks, Gina."

Several other children smiled shyly at her. Sister turned around. Gina tried as hard as she could not to smile back at the other students.

Gina finished the day and began her walk home. She was a block from the wooded area beyond her house. There had been talk among the neighbors that a Native American girl had been attacked in the woods. Lily had warned Gina to be extra careful.

Gina thought sadly, "The little girl must have been walking home from the public school on her way to her neighborhood. Or maybe on her way to school, when it was still dark. No street lights there. The trees and bushes are thick. The police were always around to bring dad home. Why weren't they around to help that little girl?"

Mrs. Lemieux's son, David, walked home slightly behind her. He and his family lived right across the street from Gina. Mrs. Lemieux kindly gave Gina and Lily wild rice every year during ricing season. Mrs. Lemieux and her family went home to their reservation and collected the rice themselves.

David pretended to bully her by throwing snowballs at her. Gina knew he was an excellent baseball player. He threw badly on purpose and missed hitting her. She knew he was there to protect her. With David nearby, no one else would try to hurt Gina. He was very shy. Gina turned to thank him when she reached her house. He took off running to the Lemieux house. She called out anyway, "Thank you, David!"

Once in the house she took off her outdoor clothes. She had to wear a scarf, cap, coat, sweaters and boots. It took a while to get everything off and put away.

"How did it go?" Lily asked. She getting ready to go to the studio to teach ballet.

Gina told her about the incident with Sister Agnes, the Lost and Found box, and Brian.

Lily hugged Gina, "You did the right thing. Somehow Sister Agnes knows she was wrong. I am so glad you were there to help Brian."

"I guess I'm glad, too. I was scared, though. I thought I would be punished."

"Sometimes standing up for other people is like that," Lily sighed. She set milk and cookies in front of Gina.

"Why do most of the Native American children live in that neighborhood down by the river? And why don't the police do anything about the little girl who was attacked? They could at least put in streetlights. And cut down the bushes," Gina said.

"All I know is some police are bad, or lazy, or I don't know. Or, don't like Native Americans. I don't understand it," Lily answered.

"Don't you have a friend who lives there?" Gina asked.

"Yes, Mary. We went to high school together. I haven't talked to her in a while. Her husband used to hit her. He finally left. Her daughter blames Mary. She thinks Mary made him unhappy. That's why he left."

"Why does the daughter blame her mother?" Gina asked in surprise.

"I don't know. Do you blame me?"

"No! It wasn't your fault. Dad was horrible."

"How could anyone hit a woman as kind as Mary?" Lily wondered.

"How could dad hit you?"

Lily looked at the clock. "Oh, Gina! Look at the time! I'll be late. Think of something nice. Do your homework. Lock the door! I'll be home later. Dinner is in the fridge. I love you!" Lily grabbed gloves and keys. She put on her coat as she left.

"Love you, mom!"

Gina locked the door. She looked at her homework. "I can go to ballet class next week. That will cheer me up."

27

———————

That Saturday Lily told Gina, "Your cousins invited us to go skiing with them."

Gina look up from breakfast with a worried look. "Skiing? I don't know how," she said.

"I know. I can't go with you. I'm teaching ballet all day. They said they will teach you."

"I can't learn to ski in five minutes!" Gina said. She remembered the day at the lake with her cousins.

"Will you try it? They really want you to be there."

Gina shrugged her shoulders, "I don't want to, but I'll go if you want me to."

Lily put an arm around Gina's shoulders, "Oh, good. I'll tell them to pick you up."

"When are we going?" Gina asked.

"Today," Lily answered.

"Today?!"

"I'm sorry, Gina. I forgot to tell you earlier."

"No, it's okay. It gives me less time to worry about skiing!"

A station wagon full of her laughing, joking cousins picked her up before noon. It was a perfect day. The sun glinted off of the snow. The blue skies were clear. There was no wind. Her aunt drove them out to a ski resort. There were several levels of hills for skiers, including some very difficult ones.

After parking, they hauled skis, poles and boots from the top of the car to the chalet. They rented equipment for Gina. All of her cousins skied regularly. They were quite good at it.

They raced off to the slopes, leaving Gina alone in the chalet. "Well, this is silly. I can't even figure out how to put the ski boots on," she muttered.

She sighed and settled on a bench. She watched out the huge picture window at the slopes.

She watched her cousin, Jeanine, tackle the hardest hill. She heard others' whispers. "Who is that? She's a daredevil! Wow, look at her go!"

Gina thought, "That's my cousin. She is doing the scariest thing I have ever seen. She's having fun doing it. I don't think I will ever do anything like that my whole life. She's so cool. And perfect. I'm too scared to even dance on a stage. And the stage is pretty flat!"

After a couple of hours, her cousin Nancy came back to the chalet. "Gina, we're getting ready to go home. Didn't you go out and ski?"

"I don't know how," Gina admitted.

"Oh, Gina! I feel terrible. Why didn't you ask us to help you?" Nancy asked. She put her arm around Gina.

"You all were so excited and rushed out right away. So, I stayed here."

"You know what? When everyone else comes in, we'll say you skied with me. I was on the easy hills. No one has seen me all day. Next time, please ask me to help. Here they are!"

Gina put on her biggest smile. She told the rest of her cousins, "I had a great time!"

Gina laughed and joked along with Nancy, Jeff, and Jeanine on the way home. Aunt Maggie invited her for dinner.

"Aunt Maggie, I'm tired. And I go back to ballet classes tomorrow. Thank you, though."

"Oh, we'll drop you at home!" Maggie suggested.

When they reached Gina's house, she waved a mitten, "Good Bye." She went into the warm kitchen.

Lily was home. "How awful was it?" she asked.

"The good thing is, there is no way I could have broken a bone skiing."

"You didn't make it to the slopes," Lily said.

"No, and it's okay. And I have ballet tomorrow after school!" Gina clapped her hands.

Lily laughed. "Thank you for going. Your cousins love you, you know."

"I do. They are cool," Gina said.

Gina was happy that school flew by on Monday. She took the bus downtown. At last she was back in ballet class with Madame. Class was harder than she thought it would be. She tired more easily.

"No jumping tonight, Gina," Madame told her. "Your lungs are not strong yet."

"Yes, Madame," Gina curtsied. She was grateful. She left class early as instructed, dressed, and took the bus home.

Gina came into the house winded from her run from the bus stop. Huffing and puffing she unwound her scarf. She took off her boots. "Mom, I can barely run anymore! I am tired. It was great to be in ballet class, though. Madame said I'll be back in shape in a few weeks."

Lily stirred a pot on the stove. "Good! Will you set the table?"

"Yes, birthday girl." Gina hugged Lily. She went off to her room to get a gift. She set the table. She placed the gold wrapped gift at her mother's place.

The phone rang. Gina answered. "Yes, grandma. It's tonight. See you soon."

She hung up. "How come grandma never says 'Hello' or 'Good Bye'? She just starts talking and hangs up when she's done," Gina asked.

"Gina, you know my mother has schizophrenia. That must be part of it."

"Well, they have a nice apartment at the senior home. And staff there that makes dinners and cleans. Does that help grandma?" Gina asked.

"Yes, I suppose so. Do you remember their old house? It is so beautiful. When are they getting here?" Lily stirred sauce on the stove.

"I remember their old house a little. It's big. Grandma didn't say when they would be here."

"I'll have everything ready for when they do," Lily said.

After a while the front door bell rang. Lily turned off the stove. She went to answer the door.

Lily hugged her parents. "We're having pasta. I hope that is okay, mom and dad."

Gina took a cake from her grandfather. She set it on the kitchen counter. "You grew, Gina! Are you healthy now?" he said, hugging her.

"Yes! All better," Gina said, hugging him. She hugged her grandmother. Gina ushered them to the table. They sat down.

Dinner was wonderful. Lily made a wish and blew out candles. She opened the gift of a mohair sweater from her parents. "Mom, did you make this? It's beautiful! Thank you!" Lily put it on immediately.

"I did. The green matches your eyes."

Lily unwrapped the gold present. "It's from me and Uncle Gene. He sent me money to buy it."

"Oh, Gina, it's perfect." Lily unwrapped a large bottle of *Joy* scented bubble bath, a matching soap, and a small bottle of *Joy* perfume. "Thank you, Gina. I'll call Gene later. Everyone, please go get comfortable in the living room. I'll bring in cake and coffee."

"And don't forget ice cream!" Gina said.

"Oh, no. Of course not."

While Lily was in the kitchen, Gina saw better how her grandmother's illness affected her.

Her grandmother leaned toward Gina. "And

you know, when my little son drowned, I didn't stop working for a day! Not a day. And so many suicides in the family. Gina, you must be careful. It all makes me so afraid."

Her grandfather took her grandmother's hand. "Don't worry. Lily will take good care of Gina."

"And I didn't take care of my son. It was my fault he drowned," she snapped. She jerked her hand away. She stood up as Lily came in with the cake.

"We're leaving. Get me my coat," she announced.

"But, grandma you didn't have any cake," Gina protested.

"I don't want any!" she snapped. She put on her coat and stomped out the door.

"I'm sorry, Lily. Thank you for dinner." Lily's father hugged her.

"It's okay, dad. We'll talk soon." She shut the door behind them.

"Gina, what happened?" Lily asked. She took a bite of cake.

"She talked about Uncle Matthew's death again. She thinks it's her fault."

Lily sighed. "I know. And it wasn't her fault. He slipped and fell into the river. No one could have saved him."

"Is that why I had to take swim lessons when I was too little? I failed them because I was scared of the deep water."

"I remember. I'm sorry about that. I thought I was helping you," Lily explained.

"It's okay. Grandma makes a great cake, though."

"Your grandfather made it. She can't do things like baking anymore."

"Oh. Well, it's fantastic! Mom, it's your birthday. What should we do? Movie?"

"Yes! *Madeline* at one of the little movie theaters. They rereleased it," Lily said.

"You love that movie!" Gina said.

Lily handed Gina a coat and put on her own. Lily and Gina both loved the story of the young orphan named Madeline. She attended a Catholic boarding school in Paris with eleven other girls.

"I love Sister Clavel," Gina whispered, munching popcorn.

"And Chef Hélène!" Lily whispered back. They settled in to see Madeline's mischievous exploits.

"Madeline always thinks everything will be wonderful," Lily murmured.

A few days later Gina answered the telephone. It was Sunday morning. Both she and Lily were at home. "Yes, I will get my mother."

"Hello, this is Lily. I see. Yes, please do what you can for my mother. I will call my brother to come home."

"Mom, what happened?" Gina asked.

"Your grandfather had a stroke and died, Gina. The paramedics tried to save him. Oh, I will miss him." She put her head in her hand and cried softly.

"I will too, mom," Gina sniffled.

Lily placed a call to Gene. He arranged to take the next flight home.

Neither Lily nor Gina slept well. Both were worried about Lily's mother. Gina tossed and turned thinking, "How can she live without him? It will be so hard for grandma."

28

Gina awakened before it was light out. She heard Lily answer the phone. "Uncle Gene must be home," she thought. She went back to sleep.

At breakfast she went into the kitchen. She asked Lily, "Did Uncle Gene call?"

"Yes. He will be here soon."

The phone rang. Lily answered.

"What? I... I don't know what to say," Lily stuttered. "Yes, my brother and I will be there shortly." She hung up.

"It was my mother's doctor. My mother died in her sleep last night."

"Oh, mom!" Gina heard the doorbell. She went to the living room to let Uncle Gene into the house.

"Gene!" Lily sobbed. "Mom died last night!"

The three hugged and cried. After changing clothes and cocoa and coffee, Gene drove them to the apartment. They sat down with the apartment staff and people from the mortuary.

Lily looked bewildered. Gene did his best to be the decision maker. Gina held Lily's hand.

"Please keep everything simple. We know they would have wanted a funeral at the Cathedral. Burial at Fort Snelling. Dad served in World War Two. Lily and I will write an announcement for the newspaper."

They had dinner later that evening at Gene's apartment. Mrs. Popova was thrilled that Gene was back. She had set out salads, cabbage rolls, and fresh bread. Gene left briefly to go to her apartment and thank her. He returned with blini pancakes and whipped cream for dessert.

"I will call dad's attorney tomorrow. We both know they left us the house. Lily, I think you should move in with Gina. I never know where I will be," Gene suggested.

"Gina, do you mind moving? I think we can keep you at our Lady of Victory for school. And you can still take a bus to Madame's studio downtown. I can sell our house. I paid for it and it's in my name. There won't be any more house payments. It will help us out," Lily said.

"Then we will do it, mom," Gina nodded.

The funeral was held the following week. Many residents and staff from the senior home were there. The cathedral was beautiful. The morning sun came in through the stained glass windows. Aunt Maggie and Uncle Robert sat with Lily and Gene. Gina sat with her cousins. They all held hands.

Gene's voice echoed from the altar. He said a few simple things about his parents' lives and their marriage. He talked about his parents' sorrow over his brother's death. He talked about how they struggled to love and raise Lily and himself.

A soloist sang *Panus Angelicus* from behind the altar. She was hidden by the screen. It sounded like an angel was singing. They had lunch in the church basement. At the end, Gina hugged her relatives. Gene dropped Lily and Gina off at home. Gina felt very sad.

"Mom?"

"Yes, Gina."

"You know all the silly stuff about being Catholic? There is heaven, right?"

"I believe there is. Your grandparents had troubles and pain in their lives. They deserve to be in a beautiful peaceful place now. I think they are in heaven."

"So do I. Night, mom," Gina said. Lily kissed the top of her head. Gina slept well, knowing her grandparents were safe.

The following weeks and months were spent packing and selling Lily's house. One Sunday they were upstairs. Lily folded summer clothes and put them in boxes.

"What if dad comes here after we move and finds new people here?" Gina asked.

"Surprise for Ted! He would deserve it if that happened," Lily said. "Do you still need your old, broken crayons and dried up paints from kindergarten?"

"No. We can throw those away. You can throw away the pictures I drew."

"No! Never! They're beautiful!" Lily exclaimed.

"Okay, mom." Gina took a bag of old pointe shoes and ribbons out of a closet. "Can you still wear these?"

"Oh, I guess I can afford new ones now."

"Mom, these shoes are shot. You couldn't possibly dance in them. Even if you put floor polish in them and dried them in the oven."

"The floor polish thing only works for one more use of the shoes. Out they go." Lily placed them in a pile with sheets and towels that had been used for too many years.

"Do you think anyone will buy our house?" Gina asked. "It's a nice little house."

"It is. I will miss Mrs. Lemieux and Mrs. Lane. Maybe that couple that came by yesterday will buy it. They are Hmong people, from Laos. The realtor told me."

"Where is Laos?" Gina asked.

"It borders China. The couple has had a difficult time. It is not easy to move to the United States and make a new life. I hope the bank tells them they can buy our house," Lily replied.

"Me, too," Gina agreed.

"I can't do this anymore. I'll go make dinner." Lily headed downstairs.

The phone rang while Lily was making dinner. She called to Gina. "Great news! They can buy our house!"

Gina ran downstairs. "Great. Hey, let's watch *Beetlejuice* again! The family in it moves into a new old house. There are nice ghosts."

Lily laughed. "I don't remember my parents' house being haunted. I always hoped it would be!"

29

Uncle Gene pulled up to his and Lily's former home and parked. Lily and Gina climbed out of the car. Gina stared at the house. She first noticed the curved glass on the rounded bay window to the side of the front steps. She breathed lightly. She took in the porch that ran across the front of the house. There was a massive oak door with a brass knocker. She looked upward past the first floor, to the second, on to the third. She finally looked up to the chimneys and the tiny windows that looked down at her from the attic.

"It's huge. I don't remember it at all. I guess I was only four the last time I was here," Gina commented.

Lily swung open the heavy door. Gene went in

first. He left them to check the lights. He would make sure the old stove worked and that the water was turned on.

Lily and Gina stepped into the entrance hall. An open wooden staircase ran up to a built in curved window seat that followed the roundness of the bay window. The window was twelve feet high. It looked into an ancient oak tree. The staircase continued up to the second floor. Beyond that it led to the third floor and finally to the attic. They explored the upper floors. They found many rooms containing old furniture covered with sheets.

Gina noticed an ancient steamer trunk with the initials DJG stenciled onto the ends. "Who is DJG?" she asked.

Lily looked away from the closet she was exploring. "DJG is for Desmond Galligan. He owned the house. After that his daughter and her husband lived in it. His grandchild lived here after that."

"How do you know all this about him?" Gina asked.

"I used to play with the costumes in the trunk when I was little. He was an actor," Lily explained.

Gina jiggled the lock. She looked around it for a key. "Maybe a key will turn up somewhere."

"I know there is one. Gene used to play with me and dress up in the costumes inside. There are both men's and women's costumes in there."

"Didn't Aunt Maggie play dress up?" Gina asked.

"Not her thing. All she wanted to do was play with dolls," Lily said.

They peeked into one of the bathrooms. It's tub had claw feet like an animal. Gina instantly liked it. She turned to Lily, "Mom, it will be fun living here, but I am almost afraid to ask. Did you find out if I have to change schools?"

"No! I forgot to tell you," Lily answered. She looked out the window. There were wildly over-grown gardens below. "There is a bus that stops on our corner. I can wait with you every morning. I'll be there waiting when you return. You can keep going to Our Lady of Victory."

Gina sighed with relief. Gina turned the glass door knob of one of the bedrooms on the second floor. The bed was so high off the floor, that it had a set of three steps up to it.

They made their way down a narrow back staircase to the kitchen. "That's great about school, mom. Why are there two staircases?"

"When people had servants they did not want to be disturbed by them. The owners of the house used the wide, open staircase at the front..."

"And the servants were hidden in the back," Gina finished the sentence. "Did grandma and grandpa do that? Did they have servants?"

"No, of course not. Your grandmother used to work for Desmond Galligan's grandson. She cleaned the house. After he died he gave the house to her and your grandfather."

"Wow, they gave grandma and grandpa a house. Why hasn't anyone been living here?" Gina wondered.

"Your grandma and grandpa loved this place, so they didn't sell it. Uncle Gene was away at university. I had the studio and you. Ted didn't want to live here. We didn't have anyone to fix things if they broke down in the house. We couldn't rent it out if there wasn't a caretaker. So, we left it," Lily explained.

They entered the kitchen. Gina examined a frame mounted on the wall. It had rows of push buttons across it. "What is that thing on the wall?"

"It was used to call the servants."

"I don't like the idea of servants. Shouldn't everyone be equal? Who would want to be a servant?"

"I agree," said Lily.

Gina looked into a cupboard. She saw a mug with the word Smitty written on it. What's this?" she asked.

"Oh, Smitty! Your grandparents used to rent out rooms on the third floor to older people. Most of them had no children or their spouses had died. Mr. Smith was one of them. We called him Smitty," Lily answered.

"Really?" Gina asked.

Gene reappeared at the door to the cellar. He had cobwebs in his hair. "Yes, we called them the Roomers. They were wonderful to me and your mom when we were growing up. I think they often did Lily's homework for her when she was at ballet class."

Lily threw a kitchen towel at him. "They did not! Well, maybe they helped me a little," she smiled.

"It reminds me of your album, *Rumours*, mom."

"Fleetwood Mack meant different rumors," Lily laughed.

Gina went into the dining room. There was a heavy, long carved wooden table with twelve chairs. The chandelier above it was covered in dust. None of the crystals shone or even glittered. Her steps made noises in the floor. "Mom, everything creaks here."

"Isn't it creepy?" Lily smiled.

Gina nodded. "I love it. Is it haunted?"

Gene said, "No." At exactly the same time Lily said, "Yes."

Lily sighed, "All right. I never actually saw anything. If I could have stayed awake all night, I'm sure I would have seen a ghost!"

"Well, grandma and grandpa didn't die in this house. Still, maybe they'll come back to visit now that we are here," Gina said.

"That would be lovely, wouldn't it?" Lily smiled.

"Yes! Which room will be mine, mom?"

"Let's go look again." Lily and Gina started up the stairs to the second floor again.

Gene called up from the living room. "I'm going to check the fireplaces and the flues. I'll call a chimney sweep to come by tomorrow. How about *Frost's* for dinner?"

"Too expensive!" Lily called back down.

"On me!" he called back.

Lily and Gina came to the landing. "Oh, all right."

"Why do you always have money, Uncle Gene? I thought you were a starving graduate student?"

He looked up from the fireplace. "Doing translations for companies that have offices in the Soviet Union pays extremely well. And of course, I invest."

"Everyone should have a brother as perfect as mine," Lily remarked. She and Gina turned to go back upstairs.

The two chimed together,

> Yesterday upon the stair,
> I met a man who wasn't there
> He wasn't there again today
> I wish, I wish he'd go away...

"Where did that come from?" Gina asked.

"I don't know, but everyone knows it," replied Lily. "Like *Miss Mary Mack.*"

They stopped to repeat the rhyme. The two clapped hands and slapped their thighs.

> Miss Mary Mack, Mack, Mack
> All dressed in black, black, black
> With silver buttons, buttons,
>   buttons
> All down her back, back, back
> She asked her mother, mother,
>   mother

> For fifty cents, cents, cents
> To see the elephant, elephant,
>   elephant
> Jump over the fence, fence, fence
> He jumped so high, high, high
> He touched the sky, sky, sky
> And never came back, back, back
> Til the Fourth of July, July, July
> You lie!

"Do you know this version?" Lily started again.

> She could not read, read, read
> She could not write, write, write
> But she could smoke, smoke, smoke
> Her father's pipe, pipe, pipe

Gene called up the stairs, "What are you two singing about?"

"Nothing!" Lily and Gina sang out together. Lily led the way into a very large bedroom with a fireplace, high ceilings, and large windows. "I thought we could have our barre and mirrors here. It has a good wooden floor."

Gina jumped up and down lightly on the floor. She stopped to sneeze several times. Even her lithe body made very loud creaking sounds. She laughed and sneezed again. "We will turn the music up loud. It will work."

Movers came and brought belongings in all afternoon. Gina, Lily, and Gene unpacked small things, clothes, kitchen stuff, towels and sheets. Gene made a reservation at *Frost's* for seven o'clock.

They raced around, dressed, and piled into Gene's car. Gina loved the restaurant. She gazed at the plush seats, the arched doorways and windows. She liked the walls of sandstone and brick, the fireplaces, the lamps, and chandeliers. It was dimly lit and wonderful.

Gene explained, "This restaurant is in the Dacotah building. It was built in 1889. There were apartments upstairs. This room used to be a pharmacy. It was turned into a restaurant later."

"Yes, Uncle Gene," Gina nodded. Gina's uncle loved reading about history, thinking about history, and talking about history. She had learned long ago to listen politely because she loved him. She looked at her menu.

"Why don't we have Roomers again, Mom?" Gina wondered.

Gene and Lily looked at each other and both nodded.

"That might be an excellent idea, Gina!" Gene exclaimed.

30

———

On Sunday morning Lily came into Gina's room with two mugs of hot cocoa. "Gina, I have made a decision. I am finally going to do it. I am going to learn how to paint."

Gina got out of bed. She put on her pale blue robe. "Walls? Some of these could really use it," she said. She pointed to places where the wallpaper was peeling. It revealed tired, chipped paint beneath.

"Oh, I hadn't noticed. I mean painting pictures. Landscapes, fruit, people, I don't know. I am going to meet my painting teacher this morning. Do you want to come?"

"Sure. Where are we going?" Gina asked.

Lily handed Gina a mug of cocoa. "She has a

studio nearby. We can walk. She is French. I don't know how much English she knows."

"Okay by me," Gina responded sipping.

Both dressed and soon they were out the door. It was cold and there was snow everywhere. The air smelled fresh, like spring was coming. The sun was bright that day. They reached the studio. They looked through the wide store front window at paintings that were for sale. Behind that they saw a circle of easels with pictures in various stages of completion.

"I can see every color in the rainbow in this studio," Lily said. She pushed the door open. Gina followed her.

"It looks like there isn't anyone here," Gina said. She walked over to the big, wide sink. It was dyed a hundred different colors from artists cleaning their brushes. There was a row of jars that held brushes and rags.

Lily called into the tiny office in the back, "Madame? It is Lily. I am here to talk to you about what I should buy for class."

An accented voice called through an open door of the office that led into the alley, "I am here, cherie. Come out. I am smooching."

"Smooching?" wondered Gina.

"Gina, come with me," Lily beckoned to the

alley. Madame was there with a cigarette in a holder. Gina figured out that, 'smooching' meant 'smoking,' in Madame's strong accent.

"You must only buy artist quality paints." She handed Lily a rumpled list. "Buy these."

Lily read the list aloud. "Cardinal red, yellow ochre, cardinal yellow, viridian green, alizarin crimson, burnt umber, titanium white, ivory, black. They all sound beautiful."

"Buy linseed oil. It will make the paint flow better. If you want color not so intense, it will make the paint thinner. And best, when you are done, the paint will dry faster," Madame recommended.

She showed Lily brushes. "You must have brushes made of hog bristle. A medium sized fan, a large flat, a few small filberts, a few medium flat, and one medium sized round. And palette knives to mix the paint on the canvas. You must buy a palette, paint cleaner for clean up, and canvas for frame. I will teach you how to stretch."

She pointed to the easels positioned around the room. "You may use an easel that is here. Soon you will want to own one for home. Good?"

"Yes. Thank you!" Lily said gratefully.

"This is your daughter, yes? Gina? I heard you say. She will make good subject for you to draw at home. Good bones in face," Madame said. She held Gina's chin and tipped her face upward. "Now, go! Before shops close."

"Yes, bye!" the two said. They hurried away to the art supply store.

Back at home, Lily spread everything out on the dining room table. "The paints are beautiful, aren't they? It makes me think. We should paint your room. What color would you like? We can go to the other kind of paint store next week."

Gina looked over her mother's paints. She selected one. "Like this. Pale blue, but with a little green. Like a robin's egg, but lighter," she decided. "Where is this Madame from? Her accent is different from Madame Branitskaya's."

Lily nodded. She picked up a letter from the table. "This Madame is French, south of France, I think. On the ocean. Oh, I forgot to tell you. I have the results of your allergy test from Dr. Halverson."

"What am I allergic to?" Gina asked.

Lily looked over the letter. "Pet hair, dust, mold, flowers, and trees."

"So, life on earth," Gina said.

"Yes, but Dr. Halverson can help you with shots. I really like him."

"So do I. He's like Uncle Gene, but you feel like

you can hug him. Only you don't, because he's a doctor."

Lily laughed. "My brother isn't exactly huggable, it's true. But a good guy."

"The best. Wait, did you say shots?" Gina asked.

"Yes. Not a big deal. You'll get one in each arm once a week," Lily answered.

"Shots of what?" Gina asked.

"Of what you are allergic to. Pet hair, dust, mold, flowers, and trees," Lily explained.

"That sounds crazy! It's all the stuff I'm allergic to!" Gina threw up her hands.

"You only get a little and your body gradually learns to not react," Lily assured her.

Gina sighed. "When do I start?"

"Tomorrow you don't have a ballet lesson downtown. You'll take the same bus. Will you be okay finding his office?" Lily asked.

"Yes. I remember from when we went to get the test. I'll be okay," Gina nodded.

"I'd go with you if I could."

"I know, mom. I can do it by myself," Gina said firmly.

31

———————

The next day Gina took the bus downtown. She went to the address her mother had given her. The office was in an old Art Deco style building in the heart of downtown. She liked the curly black iron door. Around the door were carved stone flowers. The marble floors were polished and slippery. She pressed the button for the elevator to go up. She got in, happy that she was alone. "No scary strange men," she thought.

She pressed the button for the fourth floor. She walked down a hallway and found the office. "I'm Gina Shostek. I'm here to see Dr. Halverson," she politely said to the receptionist.

She heard a boy's voice behind her. "Gina,

come sit by me. You have my cousin in your classes at Our Lady of Victory."

Gina turned. She saw a tall, slender dark haired boy waving her over. She walked past other parents with children who were there for allergy shots.

She sat down next to the boy. "Who are you? How do you know me?"

He smiled and said, "I'm one grade above you. Lisa and Linda are my cousins. I'm Danny."

Gina could not help noticing that the boy had only one hand. His left arm ended where his jacket did. Gina knew he saw her look. She mumbled, "Oh, you get allergy shots, too?" Gina sat down next to him.

"I do. I'm allergic to mold and pollen. And yes, you noticed. I have one hand. It's okay. I wouldn't have asked you to sit by me, if I thought you would be freaked out," Danny said.

"I'm not freaked out. I'm just wondering. Now I remember, I've seen you play piano at school assemblies. The tall part of the piano hides your hand. I never saw your hand or how you play. How do you do it?" Gina asked.

"There are special pieces written for pianists with one hand."

"Wow! How come?" Gina exclaimed.

"There was this guy, Paul Wittgenstein. He was a really good piano player. Then World War I began. He was drafted. He was shot in the elbow. His right arm had to be amputated. So, he started a new career as a left-handed pianist," Danny explained.

"How did he do it? Did he write the music for one handed players?" Gina unzipped her jacket.

"No. He was in a prisoner-of-war camp in Siberia. He wrote to his old teacher, Josef Labor, who was blind. He asked Josef for a concerto for the left hand. Josef wrote a concerto for Paul. After the war Paul learned the new composition by Josef and gave concerts," he told Gina.

"That's fantastic! Did people like his playing?" she asked.

"A lot of people said he played very well. For a man with one arm."

Gina looked Danny in the eye. "So, it wasn't really a compliment."

"No, but he didn't give up. He asked the famous composers Prokofiev and Strauss to write music for him. Oh, and Ravel. Ravel wrote a *Piano Concerto for the Left Hand*. That became the most famous," he explained.

"Really? They're such famous composers!" Gina said, impressed.

"How do you know what I'm talking about? None of the other kids would know these composers. Do you study music?" Danny asked.

"Kind of. My mom's a dancer. I study ballet. There's music in our house all the time," Gina explained.

A nurse appeared at the end of the room. "Danny, you can come back."

"See you after. We have to sit here for thirty minutes after we get shots. They make sure we don't have a reaction."

Gina nodded. Seconds later she was taken for her shot. Soon she and Danny were together again in the waiting room. Danny looked up from writing an English assignment in a notebook. Gina spoke. "I think you're brave to play piano for the whole school."

Danny considered. "I have eleven brothers and sisters who would do serious damage to anyone who made fun of me, so I don't know if I'm brave."

"You live in one of the huge houses across from school?!" Gina asked.

"Yep."

She whispered. "Do you know the family with the grandparents that split up?"

"Yeah. The mom and the nun? My parents told our whole family about it one night. I mean, we all already knew. My mom thought we should know so we don't judge them, I guess," Danny replied.

"And you wouldn't have judged them anyway, would you? I wouldn't," Gina admitted.

"No. Love is love," he sighed. "What happened with you and Tim?" he asked casually.

"I would rather be a ballerina than have a boyfriend," Gina answered.

"I get that. Beside playing piano, I'm a clown."

"A clown?" Gina smiled.

"For kids' birthday parties. I practiced on all of my brothers and sisters. Talk about a tough audience! They don't let anything go by, so I got to be pretty good."

"Cool!" Gina exclaimed.

Danny explained further. "I wear clown gloves, so I get to hide my hand."

"How do you hold balloons to blow them up and stuff?" Gina asked.

"With my toes," he winked.

"Really?"

"Yeah my sisters love painting my toenails. Colored toenails are part of my act. I do a few magic tricks for the kids, too."

Gina laughed. "Wow. And you're not afraid to perform?"

"Coming from a family with twelve kids? I'll take any attention I can get. Why do you ask?" Danny wondered.

"I'm terrified to dance on stage," Gina whispered.

"Imagine the audience is naked," Danny whispered back.

"I can't. I have to think about what I'm doing or I'll fall over," Gina said.

"Hmmm... Let me think on this. Hey. It's thirty minutes. We can go. Let's get a bus home." Danny deftly put on his jacket and zipped it up with one hand.

They chatted on the way home about classical music they liked. The bus bumped and swayed through the green tree-lined streets.

Danny leaned a little toward Gina. "I thought of one thing I am afraid of. I'm afraid of being liked for the wrong reason. I want to audition for a children's orchestra with my piano playing. But, I don't want them to take me because they feel sorry for me."

"Because you have one hand," Gina said. Gina glanced down at the writing on Danny's notebook.

"Yeah, but I'm a kid, too. Who wants to bad talk

and reject a kid with one hand? They would probably accept me out of pity," Danny said.

"I see what you mean." Gina looked down at the writing in Danny's notebook again. A lightbulb flashed on in Gina's mind. "The bee letter! You wrote the bee letter to me when I was sick!"

"True," Danny admitted.

"I thought I knew that handwriting. You're Mystery Friend!" Gina smiled.

Danny laughed. "Yep, it was me. Sister asked kids from other classes to write letters. Your class got tired of doing it. This is my stop. See you next week. Unless I see you at school."

"Well, thanks for the letter! You wrote the only interesting one. Bye, Danny."

Gina rode a few blocks further thinking, "What a great guy. And he can do everything! Could I ever be like that?"

That evening in the living room, Gina told Lily about Danny. "Isn't there some way he can audition for the children's orchestra, without them knowing he has one hand?"

Lily thought. "I know that sometimes classical musicians audition behind a curtain. It's so the judges don't know if it's a man or a woman. I know the person that runs auditions at Children's Theater. I wonder if they would let Danny and the group he auditions with play for them behind a curtain?"

Gina nodded. "That would work. It doesn't matter if the judges know that one person auditioning has one hand. All that matters is that they don't know which one it is."

32

The next afternoon Gina heard a small sound from the stairway. A grey striped kitten looked at her from the top one of the newel posts. "Mom! Who's that?! Is he ours?"

"I think so. I found him on the doorstep this afternoon. I asked around. A neighbor said he was from recent litter of kittens. He must have wandered off. She asked if we could take him. I wanted to surprise you," Lily explained.

Gina was already cradling the little guy. "What's his name?"

"That's up to you."

"Who's that famous Russian dancer that Madame always wants us to jump like?" asked Gina.

"Nijinsky?"

"Yes! Perfect. His name is Nijinsky. I love him. Thank you," she said, hugging both Nijinsky and Lily.

"Mom, I have the best news ever! Madame told me I can study pointe! She said I have feet like yours. And that's a good thing!" Gina hugged Lily again.

"Gina, I am so proud of you! We will get pointe shoes for you right away. I have another surprise. We have Roomers! I hope you are okay with it. We need the money."

"No, mom. That's good. Is that why there's a harp in the living room? Are they here?" Gina asked. She set Nijinsky down to explore.

"They are up on the third floor. I think you will like them. Come on." Lily led the up way the final flight of stairs. Gina and Lily recited the poem, as usual.

> Yesterday upon the stair,
> I met a man who wasn't there
> He wasn't there again today
> I wish, I wish he'd go away...

Lily knocked at the door of the largest room on third floor. An elegant elderly gentleman in a maroon paisley silk robe answered the door. A smiling silver haired lady in a deep pink kimono peeked over his shoulder at Lily and Gina.

The man smiled, "Lily! We are settling in quite nicely. And this must be Gina," he said. He offered his hand.

Gina shook it gently. She asked, "Do you play the harp?"

"That is my lovely wife, Tilly. She plays beautifully. I am Edward. I am an illusionist," he said. He flipped cards fluidly through one hand.

"Wow! You have to meet my friend, Danny. He does magic at kids' parties. And he plays the piano. All I can do is dance," Gina said.

"Your mother told us you are the most graceful young ballerina," Tilly reported.

Edward remarked, "You know the poem *Antigonish!* I heard you in the hall. By that wonderful Mr. Mearns." He and Tilly continued together.

> When I came home last night at
>   three
> The man was waiting there for me
> But when I looked around the hall
> I couldn't see him there at all!
> Go away, go away, don't you come
>   back anymore!

> Go away, go away, and please don't
> slam the door!

"That is from 1922, I believe, although he wrote it in 1910," Edward said.

"Do you know *Alibi?*" Tilly smiled and asked. She recited.

> As I was falling down the stair
> I met a bump that wasn't there
> It might have put me on the shelf
> Except I wasn't there myself.

Everyone laughed.

Lily explained, "Gina, Edward and Tilly insisted on taking rooms all the way up here. They like to look into the treetops through their windows. They have this room, the one next to it, and the bathroom. They will use our kitchen and dining room."

"Do you already have all your stuff up here? We can help you with it up the stairs," Gina offered.

"No need, my dear. Our grandson was here and gone. He brought up the heavier articles. We like using the stairs to keep us strong and young," he chuckled softly.

"The harp will stay in the living room, of course. Except when I play at the airport. Then Edward will help me load it into our van," Tilly said. She invited Gina into their sitting room. "We have made quite a start with our sitting room. Please sit."

"It's exquisite now!" Lily said in admiration. She and Gina sat on a loveseat. Edward and Tilly settled on a sofa.

European lace hung at the windows. A delicately painted Japanese screen graced part of the room. Through an open door they could see a four-poster canopied bed in the next room. Several paintings hung on the walls.

Lily went over to one painting, and then another. "Is that a Miro? And a Chagall?"

"Yes, we knew them in Paris in the twenties." Edward pointed lovingly to a photo. It was of Edward and Tilly on a bridge overlooking the River Seine. Tilly peeked out from under a cloche hat. Edward wore a fedora hat and gloves. A watch chain swung from the breast pocket of his vest.

Gina quickly did the math in her head. She blurted out, "But, you can't be that old!"

Edward laughed. He pointed to himself. "Born

1902. I'm eighty seven." He indicated Tilly, "Born 1905."

She batted her eyelashes and laughed, "I'm only eighty four."

"How wonderful that you knew Miro and Chagall? How did you meet them?" Lily politely asked.

"In a cafe'. We worked for them stretching canvases, cleaning brushes, sweeping up," Edward recalled.

Gina wandered over to a painting. "Did you want to be painters, too?"

"Not after working with them! Everyone was crazy back then. And such hard work. They were fools for their art," Tilly explained. "It was nice to work for Chagall. He was in and out of Paris. He traveled to paint in the Holy Land and Brittany. We stayed in Chagall's studio when he was gone. It was a nice place."

"And we liked his work," added Edward.

"Wow," Lily breathed. "You knew Chagall. I suppose we should let you rest. And Gina has homework."

"Yes, of course. Good evening then," Edward said.

Lily muttered all the way downstairs. "They knew Miro. And Chagall!"

The rest of the evening was peaceful. Gina finished homework, had dinner, and did her ballet lesson with Lily. Gina didn't sleep very much that night, though. Nijinsky explored every inch of the room. He jumped onto her dresser and her nightstand. He crawled above on her headboard. He settled in the crook of Gina's knee. Gina finally fell asleep smiling. She did not mind at all.

33

"Mom, you forgot to lock the doors again!" Gina called. She came into the kitchen, home from ballet class. "And there is hardly any food in the fridge. Are you okay?"

"Did I? Isn't there?" Lily asked. She entered the kitchen. "I must have been thinking about choreography."

Gina found some crackers in a cupboard. She munched on one. "Well, okay. I'll remind you next time."

Later that evening, Gina and Nijinsky checked all the locks on every door and every window. Lily noticed Gina doing this on the way from the kitchen into the living room.

"What are you doing?"

"Just making sure everything is locked," Gina smiled.

"Oh, I suppose that's a good idea. Although I have had no contact with Ted. He signed the divorce papers. Should we get an alarm system?"

Gina petted Nijinsky. "It wouldn't matter. I would still check."

"I don't think your father will come here. But, I will check the doors and windows with you."

"Okay. Can you not call him my 'father'? I don't think of him that way. How about TJ?"

"The Jerk? Yes. That's good."

"Is the divorce for real?" Gina asked.

"Yes, the divorce is done. The lawyer told me this morning. TJ does not want to pay alimony or child support. It's not worth it to try to get any money out of him. I said it was okay."

Gina looked horrified. "Do I have to spend every other weekend with him?"

"No. I have full custody of you. TJ signed papers saying he agreed."

"Maybe we don't have to be worried he comes here. Let's keep checking anyway," Gina said.

They went to each door and window on the first floor. They made sure everything was secure. Nijinsky led the way to the second floor. He had done this so many times with Gina that he knew what came next.

"It's like saying 'Good Night' to this magic house," Lily commented.

"Why is it a magic house?" Gina asked. She checked a bedroom window.

"Because the house was a big, huge, wonderful present. Your grandfather had lost his job."

"What was it like for you and Uncle Gene to move in here?" Gina asked.

"We thought we had awakened in a dream. No house is better for playing hide and seek than this! Gene and Maggie could never find me. And for seances and spirit boards!"

"You played with those? But, you don't want me to play with them," Gina said. She checked another window.

"You're more sensitive than I am," Lily replied.

"How do you know?" Gina asked.

"Because you have nightmares sometimes. You are very creative and your brain doesn't always want to sleep when you do. That's why you are good at making up stories," Lily explained.

"You mean the Gabriela stories. You made those stories up with me so I would fall asleep when I was little. They were just silly." Gina picked Nijinsky up and petted him.

"The Gabriela stories were wonderful! She traveled everywhere and did everything! Not all children can make up stories. I bet your friends can't." Lily fastened the lock of a window.

"You're right. I can't imagine Phil or Sharie making up stories," Gina admitted.

"Exactly!" Lily exclaimed.

Gina laughed. She spied something on a bookshelf in the library. "Mom, what's this? It has your name written in it."

Lily took the book and smiled, "It's *The Lady of the Lake*. Sir Walter Scott wrote it." She handed it back to Gina. "I think you would like it."

Gina flipped through the pages. "Oooh. Kings and queens and stuff. Can we act it out?"

"It's late."

"It's not a school night," Gina reminded her.

"You're right!"

Both of them set off running for the costume trunk. Gina reached it first. She flung open the lid. "Okay, who are the characters?" she asked, puffing.

"Let me think. King James. He hates the Douglas clan, especially the main guy, Douglas. There is Douglas's daughter, Ellen. A few knights."

"You said 'clan.' What is a clan?"

"Yes, it takes place in Scotland, so families are called clans."

"Like gangs?" Gina asked.

"I suppose you could call them gangs," Lily answered.

Gina took out a pale blue cape. She put it around her shoulders. "And everyone is in love with Ellen, right?"

Lily took out a tartan scarf. She put in on like a kilt. "Yes, you be Ellen. I want to be the king. For the rest of the parts, we will just switch around."

"I can switch fast," Gina agreed.

Lily nodded. They gathered a pile of clothing for costumes. Lily began leafing through the story.

She read, "When King James was a boy, Douglas took care of him. Douglas was cruel to the boy king. Douglas was jealous because he would never be king. So, King James hated all Douglasses. All Douglasses were banished from the kingdom."

Gina took the book. "Let's skip ahead."

She read, "Years later a man named Fitz wanders to Loch Katrine. A young woman, Ellen, picks him up. She takes him to a lodge."

Lily told her, "The lodge is the Douglas's hideout. Remember Douglasses are banished from the kingdom."

Gina read, "At the lodge, Fitz has dinner with Roderick, Ellen, and Malcolm. Ellen's father, Douglas is there, too. Fitz falls in love with Ellen."

"Fitz figures out the lodge is the Douglas's secret hide-out," Lily explained.

Gina asked, "Who is the Lady of the Lake?"

Lily replied, "Ellen is the Lady of the Lake. She is a naiad. A naiad is a sprit who watches overs streams and lakes. I looked it up when I was little. Look, I wrote it in the margin."

"You mean you asked Uncle Gene."

"I suppose I did. He knows..."

"Everything about everything," they chimed together.

"So, Fitz, Roderick, and Malcolm are all in love with Ellen. It's a fairy tale, so they should be!" Gina said, patting her hair.

"Exactly." Lily took the book. She glanced down at the story. "Roderick asks Douglas for Ellen's hand in marriage."

Gina took back the book. "Didn't people get married because they fell in love? Doesn't anyone care what Ellen wants?"

"Not back then. In some countries parents decide who their children will marry. Even today," Lily answered.

Gina made a face. "Marrying someone you don't know. That sounds horrible."

"Who knows, maybe my parents would have chosen better for me? I don't think they could have done any worse!" Lily laughed.

Gina looked sadly at Lily for a moment. She returned to the book and read, "Douglas will not force Ellen to marry Roderick."

Gina pointed to the page. "Good thing, too. Listen to this."

She read, "Roderick is a murderer."

Lily took the book and read, "Now Fitz asks Ellen to marry him. Ellen refuses. He gives her a ring. If Ellen shows the ring to the King of Scotland, the king will grant her wish."

"Now I remember," Lily nodded.

Lily read, "Roderick shows up and tries to kill Fitz. A whole bunch of other people are murdered. Roderick is wounded. With his bugle, Fitz calls for a doctor."

"Why didn't Fitz kill Roderick?" Gina asked.

Lily laughed, "He was a good guy."

"And Fitz just happens to have a bugle with him?" Gina laughed.

"Yes, everyone carried around bugles. To call to each other across the highlands. Fitz sets off for a festival at Stirling Castle," Lily said.

"And now Fitz is going to a party in Stirling Castle?" Gina asked.

Lily explained, "Mary, Queen of Scots became queen in Stirling Castle. Her son, James the Sixth, became king in Stirling Castle. It's an important castle."

"There's a little Uncle Gene in you," Gina smiled.

Lily continued reading, "Ellen goes to the king in Stirling Castle. She shows the king the ring that Fitz gave her. She asks the king to forgive her father, Douglas, for being cruel to the king when he was a child. Ellen sees that Fitz is really the king. The King forgives Douglas."

"What ever happened to Malcolm?" Gina asked.

Lily answered. "Malcolm is at Stirling Castle, too. Ellen and Malcolm marry. At last! A party!"

"What happened to Roderick, the murderer?" Gina wondered.

"Roderick later dies in prison," Lily said.

"So this whole story was about getting the king to forgive Douglas?! And all those people were murdered? And Ellen almost married the wrong man? Twice?" Gina asked.

Gina put the book back on the shelf. "It sounds like a big mash up of *Cinderella* and *Romeo and Juliet*. With the drug gangs at the old house in Minneapolis thrown in."

"How do you know about gangs in our old neighborhood?" Lily asked.

"Phil told me. He said that gangs sold crack cocaine on our street in Minneapolis. And that crack is new," Gina reported.

Lily looked sad. "It's true."

"I've always wondered. No houses were ever broken into on our block. No cars were stolen. Why not?" Gina asked.

"The gangs who work by our house are businessmen. They don't want the police to be called to our neighborhood. They only care about selling drugs. The dealers made sure no houses were robbed, or cars stolen. In a strange way, they protected us."

"Too bad they didn't protect the Native American girl from being hurt," Gina said.

"It is too bad," Lily agreed.

Gina remembered, "I used to see one man on Friday nights. He would drive up in a big car. He wore an amazing suit and hat. He always parked by our house. He walked to that yellow house across the street. I saw him from the window. He came before you got home from teaching. Is he scary?"

"Not to us. I saw him, too. Sometimes he came again on Saturday when you were downtown at ballet class. He delivered drugs to the dealers. And picked up money from them," Lily explained.

"He did?! Why didn't he bother us?" Gina asked.

"We don't have anything he wants. We don't want drugs. We don't have any money. Gina, I didn't know you saw him. I would have warned you. I should have anyway," Lily said.

"We had Phil for that, mom. But, that's why he and Sharie moved away. Because of the drug dealers in our neighborhood."

"I try to protect you, Gina." Lily looked anxious.

"I know, mom. It's not your fault. Anyway, we've got a play to act out!"

An hour later they sat on the floor huffing and puffing. They played all the parts. They acted, sang, and danced the entire *The Lady of the Lake*.

Gina took off the pale blue cape. She asked, "Why is it so much more fun to play boy parts? Playing creepy Roderick was way better than playing boring Ellen."

"Because men get to do everything," Lily answered. She took a wedding veil off of Gina's head.

"Is this what high school is going to be like?" Gina asked.

"You mean all the boys liking one girl, who is pretty and boring? Endless drama? Yes! That's why fairy tales are good to read. You will be ready for high school," Lily answered.

Gina laughed "You are right about the Gabriela stories. We need to write more stories with girls doing everything. Girls who do everything because they are strong."

"We certainly do need to write those." She gave Gina a wink. "I promise we will."

34

———————

The bus ride to school was longer now. Gina didn't mind. She did her homework. She gazed out the windows at the tall trees of the old neighborhoods she passed through. When she reached downtown she switched to a northside bus that took her to school. Danny was waiting for her when she got off. He grabbed her backpack strap. He spun her around.

"Gina, guess what?!" he said with a broad smile.

"You got into the orchestra!" Gina smiled. She hugged him.

"I did. And they did what your mom suggested. Everyone auditioned behind a curtain. None of the judges knew I had one hand and I got in!"

"Woohoo!!!" they both whooped.

"I have some news, too. Madame says I can start studying pointe," Gina announced proudly.

"Pointe? You mean in those hard shoes on your tiptoes? Well, congratulations!"

"We better go in. I see Sister on the steps waving to us," Gina said. She untangled herself from her backpack.

Gina felt happy all day. On her way to class she thought," I knew Danny would get into the orchestra. They wanted him for how well he played. I wish I could dance on stage behind a curtain. I suppose that wouldn't be the point. Would it? Or, maybe behind a scrim. Then I couldn't see the audience. They could only sort of see me."

Gina sat down in Creativity class. Sister Carmelita was their teacher. Sometimes she taught them drawing, painting, or sculpting. It was unusual for her to offer a creative writing lesson. She was from Italy and would only be with them for a year. Gina supposed she taught art because Sister could barely speak English. Gina and the others loved her.

Sister Carmelita usually wore a full, floor-length habit and veil. Today she walked in wearing a black habit that ended just below her knees. She wore a veil that brushed her shoulders. The students stood up and applauded and cheered.

"Sister, you finally did it! We asked you all winter to wear regular skirts like the other nuns!" a boy named Greg called out.

Sister smiled and giggled. She happily chatted away to them in Italian. She drew pictures on the board when the students couldn't understand her.

She handed out a poem. It celebrated spring. Emily Dickinson had written it. She asked Greg to read it aloud.

> Dear March
> Come in
> How glad I am
> I hoped for you before
> Put down your Hat
> You must have walked
> How out of Breath you are

She then directed them to write their own poems about spring, or about anything. Gina chose to write about daydreams.

> Daydreams
> Drift into your mind
> Unhappy days are lifted
> Bright days are made perfect
> Dreams can almost be touched

What should be now
Fashioning what can be
Rarely realized
Once so close
When done are soon forgotten

Sister smiled when she read it. Gina knew that she had done well. Gina mused, "Mom tells me that praise doesn't matter. Only what I think matters. But, I don't know, making someone else smile is nice."

At home, Gina sat at the dining room table. She was doing homework. "Homework is stupid. Filling out worksheets," she said to Nijinsky. He was lounging on a placemat on top of the table. Suddenly Nijinsky leapt from the table. He ran upstairs.

"Mouse?" Gina wondered following him. In the third floor hallway, Gina heard Tilly's voice. She was speaking to someone. Tilly was very angry.

"Take my advice, Mr. Cardomine. Go away immediately. This must be an unhappy house, Mr. Cardomine. There must be memories in every corner of it. Mr. Cardomine, just go," Tilly said.

"Who is Mr. Cardomine?" Gina wondered. She ran after Nijinsky. He had bolted into Edward and Tilly's sitting room. She found Edward holding some sheafs of paper. Tilly was seated at a small round table. She wore a turban on her head.

"Oh, I'm sorry," Gina exclaimed. "I thought someone was trying to hurt you."

"Not at all, dear," Tilly said. She stroked Nijinsky. "I am rehearsing for a play."

"You play the harp at the airport. And you are an actress, too?" Gina asked.

"Yes. Edward is also an actor. We work at various theaters. To save money for traveling we live here," Tilly answered.

"We've only just returned from working at a theater in London," Edward said. He twirled the ends of his mustache. "Our grandson lives nearby. We store our things with him whenever we are gone on adventures. He and his wife have children, so we don't live with them. Just now we each have parts at the Guthrie Theater here in *Blithe Spirit*. Do you know it?"

Edward waved Gina over to sit. Gina sat on the loveseat. "No. What's it about? Who is Mr. Cardomine?"

Tilly removed her turban. "This turban is hot! *Blithe Spirit* is a play by Noël Coward. It's about a novelist, Charles Cardomine. He invites the medium, Madame Arcati to his house to conduct a seance. He needs ideas for his next book."

"And you play Madame Arcati! A seance is when a medium talks to dead people, right?" Gina asked.

"Yes. I am Madame Arcati. I accidentally contact Charles' first wife, Elvira, who died. And I have to wear this itchy turban," Tilly complained.

Nijinsky leapt into Edward's lap. "So, Charles is haunted by Elvira's ghost. Elvira tries to ruin Charles's marriage to his new wife, Ruth."

Tilly laughed. "Only Charles can see Elvira. Ruth can't see her. Lily would be lovely as Ruth."

Gina considered. "She'd rather play Elvira. Do you believe in ghosts?"

"Oh, my. Yes! Sometimes we draw them to us," Edward replied.

"I imagine there are one or two in this house. I have heard them." Tilly waved towards the ceiling.

"I have heard stuff. Isn't that squirrels on the roof?" Gina asked. "I had a vision once. Is that the same as a ghost?"

"What did you see, dear?" Edward asked.

"I was in church. I was four years old. I saw a dove above the altar. Not a real dove, it was made of light. I looked for it again and again. I never saw it again."

Tilly thought. "I don't think that was a ghost. I

think it was the universe telling you that you are very special and loved."

"That's nice! I like that, Tilly." Gina settled farther into the loveseat.

"The ghosts we sense in this house seem sad. I'm not sure why," Tilly remarked.

Gina rose. She scooped up Nijinsky. "We should have a seance. Maybe they'll talk to us. I better go do more homework."

At the doorway, Gina turned back. "Wait! Maybe it's Galligan's ghost!"

"Who is Galligan?" Tilly asked.

"The actor who lived here. His grandson gave this house to my grandmother," Gina explained.

"When did he live?" Edward asked.

"I found some news articles in the attic on our first day here. I can't read them because of my allergies. I'll get them." Gina put Nijinsky down. She returned with a small wooden box. In it were news clippings from ancient newspapers. "This is from 1923."

Edward looked at it. "It's a press release from an Irish newspaper. It is about the silent film *Spanish Dancer*. I recall Pola Negri was magnificent in it. She was very famous."

Tilly looked over his shoulder. She read aloud, "Desmond Galligan has a large role in *The Spanish*

Dancer. We all know him as the famous child actor from our own Dublin. Born November 6, 1851, he has appeared in twenty six Hollywood films. He had important roles in *Passion Flower,* from 1921 and *Her Gilded Cage* from 1922."

"He was a big deal," Gina commented.

Edward continued reading. "The film is a lavishly produced swashbuckler set in 17th century Spain. Galligan plays Ambassador to the King of Spain. *The Spanish Dancer* is another rung for him on the golden Hollywood ladder."

Tilly took back the article. "Oh, listen. Readers may recall that Galligan was married to Kate Claxton. She was well known for playing Louise in *Two Orphans*. In 1901 Galligan claimed to have divorced Kate Claxton in the press. But, no divorce had taken place! Galligan's second wife, Frances Riley, was pregnant."

"Galligan was still married to his first wife, Kate? And he was also married to Frances! Two wives at once!?" Gina was shocked.

"Kate finally sued him for divorce and won. Hmmm... Not a good thing to do in Hollywood," Edward observed.

"Or, anywhere! When did he die?" Gina asked.

"This was written while he was still acting. I don't know," Tilly said. She rummaged through the box. "Nothing is mentioned in the other articles. It looks like he spent the rest of his career acting on stage. Mainly on Broadway. Maybe Hollywood didn't want him in the movies after he had two wives."

"Let's have a seance and try to talk to him. We play with spirit boards all the time at slumber parties!" Gina suggested.

"Wonderful! We'll ask Lily if we can hold a seance. It will be excellent research for my part." Tilly had moved to the sofa. She held Edward's hand.

"I better get back to my homework. Can we wear costumes when we have the seance?" Gina asked.

"Of course!" Edward smiled.

"This will be exciting!" Gina hugged her arms around herself.

Edward pointed to the door.

"Oh, yeah. Homework." Gina took Nijinsky and returned to long division.

35

In Dr. Halverson's waiting room, Gina sat next to Danny. He had just had his shot. He was waiting thirty minutes to make sure he didn't have a reaction. Gina waited to be called.

Gina leaned over to Danny. She said in what she hoped was a thrilling whisper, "An older couple, Edward and Tilly, live with us now. They think our house is haunted."

"Cool," Danny whispered back. "Why are we whispering?"

"So people don't think we're weird talking about ghosts," Gina said in a low voice.

Danny commented, "*The Woman in Black* is on TV. *Ghostbusters* came out a few years ago. *Ghost* is in movie theaters now. No one would think anything at all if we talk about ghosts. Ghosts are pretty common stuff."

"Oh, you're right. Anyway, we're having a seance," Gina announced.

"Gina, you have to let me come! I'll carry your books. I'll do your homework. Anything!" Danny offered.

Gina smiled. "Of course you can come. That's why I'm telling you about it."

A nurse appeared. "Gina, you can come back."

"See you in a few," Gina said getting up.

"Remember, I have my performance today," Danny reminded her.

Gina nodded. "Yes. You will be great."

After Gina's shot and a thirty minute wait, they walked to the Walker Art Center.

"It's nice you play the piano," Gina said. They watched other instrumentalists carrying in large, heavy black cases. "You don't have bring an instrument with you."

They checked in and went to the green room. They waited for Danny's entrance. He was performing in the Composers' Evening. The evening showcased new talent and never before heard music. Danny had been chosen by the music academy to play a short, light piano piece.

"I wish I could dance behind a curtain. You

know, like when you auditioned. It would be great to dance that way," Gina mused.

Danny shook his head. "Gina, ballet is a visual art. No one would see you at all."

"Exactly!" Gina exclaimed.

"What about all those tutu things?" he asked.

"I'd still wear a tutu. Just no one would see me. Are you okay not playing piano behind a curtain now?" she asked.

Danny admitted, "Yeah, I love attention. Playing behind a curtain at the audition was only so I wouldn't be judged differently than anyone else. And I wasn't. I was picked for my true talent as a pianist."

"I don't even know if I have any talent. What does it feel like?" Gina wondered.

"Like I can do what the composer needs me to do. That's all. I try to keep things from getting too complicated," Danny replied.

A stage manager announced at the door, "Places, Danny."

"Are you sure you need me for this?" Gina asked.

"To turn pages while I'm playing? Are you serious?" Danny frowned.

"Oh, yeah," Gina smiled sheepishly. "I always forget about your hand."

Danny patted Gina on the back. "That's why you're my friend."

Gina told him, "I thought you would have had one of your brothers or sisters help you."

Danny made a face. "They are way too busy. And you're better at it!"

He led the way to the wings. After a moment, Danny was announced. He took his seat on the piano bench. Gina stood next to him.

Gina looked out at the audience. She thought, "Now I see why Danny wanted me to be here! He wants me to get used to being on stage. And he's right. I'm not scared. Maybe because I'm helping Danny, I don't have stage fright?" she wondered.

Danny played beautifully. The audience clapped vigorously, led by Danny's parents. Gina gathered up his music. She followed him off stage, smiling.

"Thanks, Danny," Gina said gratefully.

"For what?" he asked.

"For figuring out a way for me to be on stage and not be scared. It's a start. I think if I'm helping someone else on stage, I'm not scared," Gina explained.

Danny raised an eyebrow. "Can't you do that with other dancers on stage? Help each other out?"

Gina laughed. "Dancers are way too mean to help each other on stage."

They exited the theater. They looked around for Danny's family. "Then why do you want to be one?" Danny frowned in confusion.

Gina leaned against a wall in the lobby. "Sometimes, I don't know why I want to be a dancer. But, then I dance. Then I am more sure about being a dancer than I am of anything."

Danny leaned over and expertly retied his shoe. "I'm studying Rene Levande. He is a one handed magician. I am learning his illusions. I want to do a whole magic show."

"Maybe Edward can help you! Danny, are you afraid of anything?" Gina asked.

Danny stood back up. "Not really. The worst has already happened," he said. He nodded to his arm. "Thanks for helping me, Gina. My brother and I will pick you up tomorrow at noon."

"What for?"

Danny said, "My mom will call your mom. It's a birthday party."

"Do I get to be a clown?" Gina asked.

"No, most of my magic is ready. You will be a magician's assistant! Here's my dad. I have to get home and practice my illusions. Is your mom here?" Danny took his music from Gina.

"Yes, she can take me home. See you tomorrow!" Gina waved.

Gina joined Lily in the lobby. Lily exclaimed, "Danny was wonderful! You looked beautiful on stage, Gina. The lighting loves you."

Gina laughed. "Mom, can I go to a birthday party with Danny tomorrow? He's going to do magic. I'm going to help."

"That's a great idea. Should we go out for pizza?"

"Yes!" They left the theater and headed for a pizzeria down the street. It was a perfect day.

The next day Danny and his brother picked her up at noon. They drove to a beautiful, large home in one of the suburbs. Gina helped Danny with his suitcases and bags.

"Danny and Gina, have fun. I'll be back in an hour and a half." Danny's brother smiled. He pulled out of the driveway.

The birthday boy's mother set them up in a den off the living room. They could get everything ready there. About twenty kindergarteners were outside playing games, yelling, and laughing.

Gina set down a cage containing Danny's rabbit. "I am being careful with your rabbit. What is his name again?"

"Harry Houdini," Danny said. "Here's your costume." Danny handed her a wig, dress, and apron.

"My what?" Gina asked in surprise.

"Your costume. You are a silent cleaning lady. You come on after the third illusion," Danny told Gina.

Gina protested, "Danny, no. I don't know how to act! I thought I'd be handing you stuff."

"You don't have to say anything. Plus, you will be dressed up as an old woman. You won't be scared," Danny promised.

"What do I do? Do I get sawed in half?!" Gina asked in delight.

"No, sawing in half takes a lot of practice and a special box," Danny answered.

Gina looked confused. "A special box?"

Danny explained, "Yes, magicians don't actually kill people and bring them back to life. Anyway, you sweep me off of the stage with your broom. That gives me time to get ready for the next illusions. Then you sweep the floor. You get rid of all the confetti and fake flowers that I used in the beginning of the show."

Gina nodded. "I can do that."

"Then you come back to the den and put this on." Danny took out a tutu and tiara. "You come back onstage and help me with the final illusion!"

"You're making me be a ballerina so I get over stage fright as a dancer!" Gina smiled.

"Yes, I am!" Danny laughed.

"Oh, all right. I'll do it. It's not like I have to dance. Why do you have a tutu?" Gina wondered.

"I have sisters. It's from a Halloween costume. She was a vampire ballerina." Danny put the tiara on Gina's head.

Danny went out to get everything ready. Gina put on the wig, old dress, and apron. The children raced in. Danny directed them to sit on the floor. He wore white gloves. One covered a prosthetic hand. The children never knew that he had one hand.

After three illusions, Gina appeared as the cleaning lady. She swept Danny away. The children laughed when she batted at him with the broom. She liked the sound of them laughing. She disappeared and Danny returned.

Putting on the tutu, she realized something. "I can't see my feet!" she thought. "Wow, it's even different to walk."

She went out and assisted Danny. He made his family's rabbit disappear and reappear. Harry Houdini escaped. Gina chased and caught him. It was a hit with the children. They went wild clapping. Danny and Gina quickly went back into the den. They packed up.

"I think we will keep the part where Harry escapes," Danny said. He stuffed props in bags.

"Good idea, the kids loved it," Gina said. She quickly folded her costumes and packed them.

The children's mother came in. She gave Danny some money. "Thank you, Danny and Gina. It was fantastic!" She smiled and returned to the children.

Danny handed Gina half of the money. "Danny, no!" Gina protested. "You learned all of the illusions and got all the costumes and props together."

"A third?"

"And your brother drove," Gina reminded him.

"A fourth, then."

"Deal." Gina took the money Danny offered her. "I'll use it for new tights."

The mother had served the children cake and ice cream. Gina glanced at the children as they walked out to the car. Once outside she said, "I hate watching them eat."

"I know. It's disgusting. Best thing about having one hand? Never had to take care of younger siblings."

Danny's brother opened the car doors. He

helped with the suitcases. "How did it go Septimus?" he asked.

"Great!"

"What's Septimus?" Gina asked.

"Septimus means you are the seventh child born in your family. Like me."

"Cool! Can I call you that?"

"Not at school."

Gina got out at her house. "Thanks, you two! And Harry Houdini!"

She ran into the house. "Another great day," she thought. She called out to Lily, "Mom, it was really fun!"

36

One night Gina and her mother had class in the large bedroom that had become their studio. They had painted it a soft cream color. The room was further colored by Lily and Gina dancing. Their images were doubled in the mirrors.

After ballet class, Lily put on some Latin music. She taught Gina to salsa dance. "Mom, this is fun, but why are we doing this?"

"To remind you that you dance with your hips, not with your feet," Lily explained.

Gina frowned. "Not just salsa dance?"

Lily replied, "All dance, even ballet. Think about this. The five positions in ballet are not positions of your feet."

"They are positions of my hips!" Gina realized.

"Exactly," Lily said, sipping water.

They discussed the recital for Gina's ballet school. It was fast approaching. Gina sat on the floor sipping water. She explained to Lily, "The older girls will perform *The Fairy Variations* from *The Sleeping Beauty*. Each fairy has three young ballerinas that play fairy helpers. I'm one of the fairy helpers of the Fairy of Grace. Madame told me last night."

"I know! She called and asked if it would be all right with me. Of course, I agreed. I've been waiting for you to tell me about it. Why did you wait?" Lily asked.

"I think because I'm scared. And I told you I'll start studying pointe soon," Gina replied.

"Yes, we talked about that. You are quite strong and you are ready. It's okay to be scared," Lily admitted.

Gina confessed, "The other girls already hate me because I am younger than they are. When I can study pointe with them, they will be worse."

Lily thought for a moment. "I'm sorry to say that is part of ballet. Jealous girls. We'll go to Grand Jete' soon and have you fitted for shoes. Let's go to your room. I'll tell you about your part."

In Gina's room, Lily took out a book about *The Sleeping Beauty* ballet. She brought in a tray of cookies and milk and curled up on a loveseat. Gina sat on her bed.

Lily opened the book. She explained, "The Sleeping Beauty, Princess Aurora, is given gifts by fairies. The Fairy of Grace gives her the gift of honesty. She wears pale gold, silver, and white."

"Oooh, my costume will be pretty," Gina said.

"Yes, especially with your dark hair and green eyes. I'm sure Madame thought of that when she cast you," Lily added.

She read further. "The second fairy is the Enchanted Garden Fairy. Her gift is beauty. She wears a brightly colored tutu. The Fairy of the Woodland Glade is third. She wears green and gold. She gives the gift of generosity." Lily paused to take a bite of cookie.

She continued, "The fourth fairy is the Fairy of Songbirds. She wears yellow. Her gift is a melodious voice. The fifth fairy is the Fairy of Golden Vine. She gives the gift of passion. She wears red and gold. Last is the Lilac Fairy, the queen of the fairies. She is supposed to give the gift of wisdom to Princess Aurora. Before she can give the gift, an evil fairy curses the princess."

"And the Lilac Fairy wears lavender. Who is the evil fairy?" asked Gina, sipping milk.

"The Fairy of Revenge, Carabosse, is the evil one."

"Okay, but what is the story?" Gina asked.

"Yes, you should know the whole story. We are both dancers. As I tell the story, let's both act out parts," Lily suggested.

"But I only do the one little part," Gina said.

Lily looked at Gina. "Yes, but it is best to know how the other characters dance. You need to know what is happening around you, as you do your part. Someday you will be cast in the other roles."

"Okay. We need costumes." Gina leapt up. She went to the costume trunk in the closet. She opened it. "Who are the other characters? What do we need?"

"Stuff for the king, queen, Princess Aurora, Lilac Fairy, five fairies, and Carabosse. Oh, and Prince Florimund."

Gina took out tutus, wings, crowns, capes, and riding boots for Florimund.

Lily continued, "Then there are Blue Bird, Puss in Boots, Little Red Riding Hood and the Wolf, Cinderella, and Prince Charming."

"People from other fairy tales are in it?" Gina asked. She poked her head out of the closet.

"Madame wants to have as many people taking parts in the ballet as she can. So, a lot of characters dance in the wedding scene. I'm sure that's why she chose this version," Lily told her.

"Okay, well here are cat ears from Halloween, some blue feathers, a red hat, a werewolf mask, from Halloween, too, and another crown," Gina said. She tossed things out of the closet.

The two tried on and tossed off bits of costumes.

Lily read, "The King and Queen celebrate the birth of their daughter, Princess Aurora. The Lilac Fairy and the rest of the good fairies come to the party with gifts for the newborn princess. Suddenly, the evil fairy Carabosse interrupts the party. Carabosse is furious. The king didn't invite her."

Lily quickly dressed all in black. Lily read the Carabosse part in a raspy, cackling voice. "Aurora will prick her finger with a spindle. She will fall asleep. Aurora will sleep for a hundred years. She can only be awakened by the kiss of a prince."

"What's a spindle?" Gina asked.

"A spindle is a needle used for spinning thread. It's sharp," Lily answered.

Gina had changed into a king's costume. She announced, "I forbid spindles in my kingdom!"

Lily turned the page and read, "The king throws Carabosse out of the party. He banishes her from the kingdom. Years go by. Aurora is sixteen years old. At her birthday party four princes come to ask her to marry them."

Gina dressed as Aurora. Lily took out a box of Barbie and Ken dolls. "Here, we'll use Ken dolls for the princes, and Barbies for the fairies," she said. She set them in a row.

Gina danced with each Ken in turn, laughing. Lily put a red cape over her Carabosse costume. She gave Gina a bouquet of roses. A sharp pencil was hidden inside the bouquet.

"Is the pencil supposed to be a spindle?" Gina asked.

Lily nodded and read from the book, "Fascinated by the flowers, Aurora dances with the bouquet. Suddenly, Aurora pricks her finger on the spindle and falls to the ground."

Gina dropped to the floor, laughing. "Ow! Sorry, I fell on one of the Kens."

Lily took off her cloak and revealed that she was Carabosse.

Gina read from the floor, "The four princes attack Carabosse."

Lily grabbed the Ken dolls. She made them attack her. She said, "Carabosse puts a spell on everyone in the kingdom. They all fall asleep."

Gina put all the dolls face down on the floor.

Gina continued reading, still laughing. "Then Carabosse disappeared."

Lily jumped into the closet. She reappeared in purple as the Lilac Fairy. She danced around the room.

Lily took the book from Gina. She read, "A hundred years have passed. Prince Florimond is hunting in the forest. The Lilac Fairy appears. She guides him to the garden where Aurora rests."

"Isn't Aurora a hundred years old?" Gina asked.

"I guess the spell froze everyone in time. No one got any older," Lily said.

Gina thought. She said, "Keep being the Lilac Fairy. Make one of the Kens be Florimund. Have him come over to Aurora."

Lily picked up a Ken doll. She had him kiss the sleeping Aurora. Gina burst into laughter. "Aurora, you're supposed to be asleep," Lily said. She waved the Ken doll over Gina.

Gina told Lily, "You have to read. I can't stop laughing."

"Well, it's okay to laugh now. You were just awakened by a prince. The entire kingdom wakes up. The Prince asks the King and Queen for Aurora's hand."

Lily and Gina raced around. They set up all of

the dolls. Lily posed Ken sitting on the floor. "Gina stand up. Florimund's knees don't bend. He can't get down on one knee. He'll have to propose like this."

Lily took a ring from Gina's jewelry box. She put it on Gina's finger. Gina put on a white veil. She held fake flowers.

Lily read, "The wedding of Aurora and Florimund takes place in the palace. Many guests dance for the bride and groom."

Gina held Florimund's tiny Ken-hand. She dutifully kissed him after Aurora became his wife.

Lily directed Gina. "Aurora and Florimund dance a Grand Pas de Deux. They express the happiness that unites them."

After their dance, costumes and dolls flew. Blue Bird, Puss in Boots, Little Red Riding Hood and the Wolf, Cinderella, and Prince Charming were made to dance for the couple.

Lily read the final page. "The struggle between good and evil was over. The power of love overcame all obstacles."

"Just like in real life?" Gina asked. Her voice was slightly muffled. She was pulling the princess costume off over her head.

"Hmmm... sometimes," Lily said. She wriggled out of the Lilac Fairy tutu.

Gina started to pick up the dolls to put them away. "Why do I have six Ken dolls?"

"Because you have six Barbie's. I wanted things to be equal," Lily said from the closet. She was putting costumes back into the trunk.

"That's silly, mom. But, I like it."

"I think we need popcorn. And maybe a movie?" Lily suggested.

"Yes! Maybe not Disney though. I've had enough princes and princesses and fairies for one night," Gina answered. She trailed Lily down the stairs.

37

Gina loved rehearsing to be the friend of the Fairy of Grace. She especially loved her pale gold, silver, and white tutu and bodice. Of course, she was not allowed to rehearse while wearing it. She had had one fitting. One day after class she wore it for a few minutes. The seamstress pinned it to conform to her shape.

The weeks wore on. With each passing day Gina felt more nervous about the recital. The other girls seemed calm and confident at rehearsals. Gina pretended she didn't feel sick. Lily ran her through her part every day outside of regular rehearsals.

"Gina, it's perfect. You know the part. You will

not forget once you are on stage," Lily reminded her.

"One more time," Gina insisted, puffing.

"All right, but then you have to stop. You can be over rehearsed, you know."

Gina finished. They sat on the floor drinking water.

"Gina, you have practiced your part many times with me. You are lovely each time," Lily said. "I'm sorry I don't know how to help. It's not fair that I feel comfortable on stage. Do you know why you feel frightened about the recital?"

Gina shook her head, "I don't think I do. I just know I am."

"I will be there in the front row. Does that make it better?"

"Yes."

"I can be at final dress rehearsal tomorrow if you like," Lily suggested.

Gina sipped. She said thoughtfully, "No, that's okay. I'll be all right. It's not the real show."

At last it was the day before the performance. Gina prepared for her first final dress rehearsal. At last her time to go on stage arrived. She went to her wing with the other girls. She leaned over to tuck in the elastic tie on her shoe. She missed her cue. She went on anyway, at the wrong time.

Rattled, she got off on the wrong leg. She panicked. She knew she didn't match the other girls. She tripped slightly, trying to get back on the right step. She looked with horror at a hole in the front row of dancers. "That's where I should be now!" She raced up to the front row. She crashed into another girl on her way. She apologized. Finally she was back on track.

She raced off stage. She found Madame. "I am so sorry, Madame! I ruined your ballet."

Madame laughed. "Gina, You did not. It is rehearsal! Don't be scary on stage. Audience will know if you not have fun."

"Yes, Madame," Gina said. She returned to the dressing room to change and go home.

Gina thought, "I know she doesn't mean I'm scary. She means I shouldn't be scared. Fun! Fun? Who ever thought dancing on stage would be fun?" Gina looked at the other girls and boys. On stage they rehearsed their dances with smiles and excitement.

"They are having more fun than I ever dreamed of. Why can't I be like that?" she asked herself. She received no answer.

"I was awful!" she said arriving home.

"Bad rehearsals are okay. That's why we rehearse. Here, something to take your mind off of it." Lily handed her a delicate parchment envelope.

Gina opened it. "It's an invitation. To a seance! I have to call Danny. It's tonight!"

"Yes! Read the costume suggestions to him. Then he will know what to wear," Lily called out. Gina raced to the phone.

"Danny, it's tonight! The seance! Wear blue, stripes and florals are good. And checks and plaid. Wear something metal. Eleven thirty. Can you come?" Gina waited.

Danny checked with his mother. "She said 'Yes.' She said your mom already called her. See you tonight!"

Gina raced up the stairs. She found Lily helping Edward and Tilly prepare for the seance. The room was filled with herbs and candles. Lily was putting chairs around a table.

"Danny can come! Edward and Tilly, I had a horrible dress rehearsal!" Gina announced.

"The only good dress rehearsal is a bad one," Tilly said. She hugged Gina to comfort her.

Edward added, "Why entire Broadway shows have been shut down because a dress rehearsal was good!"

"Really?" Gina opened her eyes wide.

"Yes!!!" Tilly, Edward, and Lily said together.

"Gina, come with me. We have to work on our costumes," Lily said. She lead her out of the room.

Gina followed her. She skipped. "This is going to be so fun!"

38

———————

At eleven thirty Danny was dropped off by his oldest brother. "I have permission from my mother to stay up past midnight and spend the night, Mrs. Shostek," he dutifully announced. He entered the house. He was sporting a blue and white striped shirt, a checked tie, and blue jeans.

Lily smiled, "I already called her and checked. Thanks Danny. Great costume."

"Hi, Danny!" Gina wore a pale blue floral dress. Lily also wore a blue floral dress like Gina's. "Mom made them for us," she announced.

"Cool!"

Danny pulled up the hem of his jeans slightly. He revealed flowered socks. "They're my sister's," he whispered. "Don't tell anyone. Oh, and my gold First Communion cross for metal."

"Perfect! Let's join the others." Gina and Lily floated up the stairs with Danny up to Tilly and Edward's sitting room.

Tilly wore a blue and purple paisley kimono and turban. She invited them to sit at a round table. She poured tea for each of them. Danny remarked to Tilly, "I thought you'd be wearing a pointy black hat."

"Tilly is a medium, not a witch," Lily said.

Danny nodded. "Oh, yeah. I guess I'm a little nervous. Mostly excited. Where should I sit?"

Tilly counted. "We need one more chair. Wait, I know. We will move the table closer to the piano. Danny, you sit on the piano bench facing the table. It's the only way everything will fit in the room."

Gina asked, "Isn't that the piano from the back corner in the downstairs hallway? How did you get it up here?"

Lily answered, "Edward and Tilly hoisted it on their backs and carried it up the stairs. You've seen how young and strong they are!"

"They did not! Besides, it would never fit around the corners on the landings," Danny said.

Edward wore a navy pinstripe suit. He lit blue

and violet candles scented with cinnamon, frankincense, lemongrass, sage, clove, ylang ylang, and a dash of sandalwood. "Lily noticed that Tilly enjoyed playing. She had someone come and hoist it on a rope up the outside of the house. He placed it here."

"While you were at school," Lily added. "I forgot all about the piano after that."

"Those candles smell good," Danny sniffed.

"All of the scents open psychic channels," Edward informed him.

"And the tea," remarked Tilly. She settled the teapot back on its trivet. "It's made from mugwort. Mugwort helps us communicate with the dead. It protects us against evil spirits. I added rue so we can hear messages more easily."

"What is on the table?" Lily asked.

Tilly arranged yellow apples with their roots attached in a bowl. "This is mandrake, also know as May apples. It draws spirits near."

Danny became excited. "I know this! When mandrake is pulled out of the ground, its roots scream in agony. Any human who hears the scream dies, or goes crazy." He frowned, "How did you get this mandrake?"

Edward replied, "To harvest mandrake safely,

we borrowed the neighbor's dog, Bandit. He dug it up, while we covered our ears."

A framed photograph of Desmond Galligan stood on the table. "I found this is the box with the news articles," Gina said.

Tilly held out her hands. "Necromancers, let us sit."

Lily turned out the lights. Only the candles illuminated them. There were wonderful mysterious dark corners in the room. "What is a necromancer?" she asked.

"One who communicates with the spirits. Do we all agree that we are trying to reach the spirit of Desmond Galligan?" Tilly asked.

They all sat at the table. Everyone nodded.

Tilly warned, "It is dangerous to contact the spirits. An evil spirit might pretend to be Desmond Galligan and bring evil to the earth. We don't want to do that."

"How do you know all of this, Tilly?" Lily asked.

"I've been researching seances for my part in *Blithe Spirit,*" Tilly replied.

"Is that why we have the tea and candles and mandrake?" Danny asked.

"Yes, those things help us communicate. They also protect us," Edward nodded.

"I remember I read in the news articles that he was born in 1851," Gina reported.

Danny calculated, "Desmond would be a hundred and thirty eight years old if he was alive. He's definitely been dead for a while. Have any of you ever sensed that he is evil?"

Tilly, Edward, Lily, and Gina shook their heads. "No, we have sensed only sadness in the house, not evil," Tilly reported.

"I suppose that's good then? I would like to know what happened to Desmond. Why do the articles stop after 1923?" Lily wondered.

"I wonder what happened to him, too. Hold hands everyone. Gina and Edward, put a hand on each of side of Danny. He will need to have his hand free. Danny, you will operate the spirit board," Tilly directed.

"Why Danny?" Gina asked.

"Did you tell Danny anything about Desmond?" Tilly asked.

"No, not really," Gina answered.

"Then he knows the least of us about Desmond. We can trust Danny is not moving the pointer on the spirit board on purpose," Edward explained.

Gina placed her hand on Danny's wrist of the arm without a hand. Edward placed a hand on his other shoulder. Danny placed his hand on the pointer on the spirit board.

Tilly breathed deeply. "Everyone, think only about Desmond. Together we ask the spirits this night. Send us only the blessed and bright. We claim protection for everyone here. No evil beings can come near."

Tilly took another breath. "Tonight we are here to contact the spirit of Desmond Galligan. Desmond, please make your presence known."

A breeze entered through an open window. It caused the candles to flicker. The table cloth fluttered.

"Desmond, are you here?" Tilly asked.

The pointer on the spirit board moved under Danny's fingertip to, "Yes." Everyone gasped.

"Danny, did you move the pointer?" Gina accused him.

"No! I swear on my Communion cross!" he exclaimed.

"Desmond, what happened to you after 1923?" asked Tilly.

The pointer moved erratically over the board.

"Maybe he can only answer 'yes' or 'no' questions?" Edward wondered.

"Did you die from an illness?" Tilly asked.

The pointer moved to 'No.'

Danny asked, "Were you murdered?"

"Danny!" Gina exclaimed.

"It's what we're all thinking! I just asked for us," Danny insisted.

The pointer circled the board and rested again on, 'No.'

"So, not illness, not murder. Desmond, did you die from natural causes?" Tilly pressed.

Lily's tea vibrated in its cup. There was a far-away crackle of lightning. A very loud crack of thunder followed. A strong wind tore through the open window. It put out the candles. Rain began.

Tilly and Edward began to sing together with a melody from the piano.

> There was a boy, a very strange en-
> chanted boy
> They say he wandered very far,
> very far
> Over land and sea

One of the teacups crashed to the floor. Gina jumped. Lily smiled delightedly.

"Gina, ease up! You're breaking my arm!" Danny exclaimed.

"Oh, sorry." Gina lessened her grip. Tilly and Edward continued singing.

> One magic day he passed my way
> And while we spoke of many things,
>   fools and kings
> This he said to me

For a moment the room was lit up by lightning. It went dark again. Tilly and Edward stopped singing. There was another deafening crack of thunder. The curtains were soaked. The wind slapped the curtains against the window pane. The rain fell harder. There was silence all around. No one breathed.

Everyone heard a whispered voice. "The greatest thing you'll ever learn, is just to love and be loved in return."

"Who whispered that?" Tilly asked.

"I didn't. Not me. I was sipping tea. I didn't, either. Not I," all answered.

Lily relit the candles on the table. "Danny, play the song again on the piano. I remember it now, it is so lovely. Eden Abez wrote it. Nat King Cole sang it."

"Again? I didn't play it," Danny protested.

"But, we all heard the piano," Lily said.

"I couldn't have. I had my hand on the pointer the whole time. I couldn't have turned around to face the piano, either. Gina and Edward had their hands on me. Did you take your hands away?" Danny asked.

No," Gina and Edward answered.

"I swear. I didn't play. Besides the music is for two hands. And I don't even know the song! I'll prove it to you," Danny said.

Danny got up from the bench. He sat down again facing the piano. To his surprise he played a one-handed *Nature Boy*. "How did I play that?! I told you I don't know it. I've never even heard it before!"

"I don't know. Somehow you did. The greatest thing you'll ever learn, is just to love and be loved in return," Gina repeated.

Gina looked around at everyone. "Why would Desmond give us that message? Besides, the nuns told me you have to love yourself first. Only after that you can love other people."

Danny relaxed. He looked at his hand with new eyes. "Well, 'just to love' can mean loving yourself first," he offered.

"Why did the nuns tell me I have to love myself first? It messes with my head!" Gina complained.

"Nuns are good at that," Lily remarked.

"What?" Gina asked.

"Messing with your head!" Lily laughed. Everyone joined in.

"I think the nuns care about you, Gina," Lily said.

"I think you're right, mom. But, I don't think that the nuns would like that we had a seance."

"Maybe they would? Who knows what shenanigans the nuns get up to in that old convent. I bet they sneak sacrificial wine." Danny grinned.

"Like you altar boys do?" Gina laughed.

"Only once! Or, twice. Really, just to see if I could get away with it," Danny answered honestly.

Edward changed the subject. "Desmond wandered far with his acting. He was famous as a child. And the song is titled *Nature Boy*. About a boy who is a little shy and sad of eye, but very wise. Danny, I wonder if in future you will wander very far over land and sea."

"Perhaps he will. Please, join hands once again," Tilly directed. "We thank Desmond for visiting us and wish him well."

She blew out the candles to end the seance. Edward lit some copal incense.

"It smells like church," Danny sniffed.

"It is copal. It is burned in Catholic mass. It is for protection. If there are any unwanted spirits lurking about. And for good measure a little holy water." Edward sprinkled a bit around the room.

"Plus, now we know we won't attract vampires," Danny said. He helped move the chairs back into place.

"Were you worried I'm a vampire?" Gina asked. She stacked teacups.

"You're pretty pale. You never know," Danny laughed. He took the holy water from Edward. He gave Gina a sprinkle.

"Gina did not burn into ashes, even a little. So, I think we know she isn't a vampire. Enough spirit things. To bed!" Lily waved them out of the room.

They left, leaving Tilly and Edward reading over the news articles about Desmond Galligan.

On the stairs Gina asked Danny. "Will you be scared sleeping alone in a bedroom?"

"Are you kidding? The seventh kid out of twelve? I've never slept alone in a room before in my life!" Danny exclaimed.

Lily brought each of them cocoa to have in their rooms and went to hers. "Good Night. Sleep in. It's Saturday tomorrow. I'll knock when it's breakfast."

"Thanks, Mrs. Shostek," Danny said.

"Night, mom."

Lily continued on to her room.

Gina started to close the door to her room. She

turned back to Danny in the hallway. She asked, "Should we keep the seance a secret?"

"Yes! If my family asks, I'll say no spirits showed up. We watched scary movies with your mom all night."

"Deal," Gina said, shutting her door.

39

The day of Gina's recital arrived. Lily dropped her at the theater. Gina went into a large dressing room. She put on makeup and her costume. The other girls chattered excitedly while they got ready.

A stage manager appeared. He read a list of names, including Gina's. "Five minutes," he announced.

Gina walked down the hall. She waited in the wings with the Fairy of Grace and her fairy friends. Suddenly she felt faint. She ran out of the backstage area to a restroom. She was sick. She knew she had missed her cue. The rest of the girls were on stage dancing. She went to the dressing room and changed. "This is horrible. How could this happen?" she wondered. She was shaking. "I'm not sick. What is wrong with me?"

She raced out of the theater. Lily found her outside sitting on the steps.

Gina cried, "I was sick! I didn't know what to do! I'm awful. I should never have tried to be a ballerina!"

Lily put an arm around her. "It was the adrenalin from being frightened. It makes you nauseous. You couldn't have known that. It's okay! There will be other times. I promise. Next time we will practice helping you relax before you go on stage."

"Mom, I don't ever want to do this again. Ever." She dried her eyes. "What do I tell Madame? She will hate me!"

"I already told her that you became ill. I saw that you didn't appear on stage with the other dancers. I came backstage. I saw you leaving the restroom and walk to the dressing room. I thought you would want some time alone. Madame understands! This has probably happened to her," Lily explained.

"Can we go home?" Gina asked.

"Yes. Let's think about something else on the way." Lily offered her a hand and Gina got up.

"What?"

"Mmm... The Pride Parade is coming up," Lily suggested.

"We can plan our costumes!" Gina smiled.

They walked to the car and Lily drove them home.

When they reached home, Gina grabbed Nijinsky and went up to her room.

"I'm going to look for costume stuff for Pride," Gina said.

Gina saw the box with news articles from the seance. Edward and Tilly had returned it to Gina's room. She went up to the attic to put the box away. In the attic she looked around.

She thought, "We still don't know what happened to Desmond. There must be another article somewhere."

She looked at the dusty, old box again. Gina opened it and sneezed. She discovered an extra tray at the bottom. She lifted it out. "There is another article about Desmond!"

She read, "Desmond Galligan died on October 29, 1929 in New York City, a day after the Black Monday stock market crash. He is survived by his wife, Frances, and daughter, Kate. It is believed Mr. Desmond took his own life."

Lily came up to the attic. She found Gina crying. "Here you are! What's wrong?"

"Look at this," Gina said. She showed the article to Lily. "Desmond Galligan took his own life! Mom, people who go on stage have horrible lives. Mr. Galligan killed himself. He was on stage all the time! I don't want to be a dancer!"

Lily looked at the news article. "This is so sad about Mr. Galligan. Gina, Mr. Galligan died right after the stock market crashed. He may have lost all of his money. He was seventy eight years old. Maybe he was sick, too. He might have taken his life because he was old and broke. I don't think he died because he had been on stage. We'll never know for sure."

Gina sniffled. Lily gave her a tissue and she blew her nose.

"Is Desmond's death what you are so upset about? Is there anything else?" Lily put an arm around her.

"Mom, I can't dance anymore! I'm too awful! I got sick!" Gina sobbed.

Lily held her. "It is okay to feel this way and let tears happen. But it is not true. You are an excellent dancer." She handed Gina another tissue.

"How can I feel awful and not believe I'm awful? I must be awful! And I still miss Pepe and Sharie and Phil. And grandma and grandpa. I can't get over all of them not being here." Gina dabbed at her nose.

Lily assured her. "It is good that you miss them. It means you love them! You feel like dancing was taken away from you today. You are missing dancing, too. That might be how you feel right now. I know you have a huge talent in you."

"Maybe," Gina said looking up.

Gina frowned. "Why can't I be like other kids? Phil and Sharie aren't like this! They do normal kid stuff. They're happy! You're an artist, mom. You're not happy!"

Lily took Gina's hand. "It's true. Sometimes I'm very sad. But, being an artist is what helps me to be happy. Sometimes, everyone is unhappy. We are human. Our goal is not to feel happy all the time. It is just to feel."

"I thought it was just to love? Like Desmond's message?" Gina asked.

"To love, too. Sometimes to hurt," Lily admitted.

"Mom, I hate hurting! I hate crying! It doesn't matter, anyway. I can't go on stage. I can't be a ballerina." Gina sniffled.

"Gina, this is part of becoming a ballerina. Sometimes a ballerina feels she can't go on stage.

That will change. What about Danny? Does he have stage fright?" Lily asked.

"Danny? He loves being on stage! And he's my friend. He's always learning how to do new stuff that he's afraid of!" Gina exclaimed.

"That's true. He does. Danny can help you. And so will I. And for now, you need to think about something fun. Ballet will be there when you are ready again." Lily smiled at Gina.

Gina was up now and twirling around the room. "Can we ask Danny to go to the Pride Parade with us? Let's get out of this dust before I... Achoo!"

Lily and Gina went down the stairs. Tilly and Edward's door was open. They waved them in.

"I got sick at the recital and ran away," Gina announced. "And Desmond committed suicide!"

"As for the recital, your body told you that you were not ready to dance in that moment. You will be later my dear," Tilly said. She hugged Gina for an extra long time.

Edward rose to make tea. "And by then, the world might just be ready for your dancing. Come, sit down."

Tilly mused, "Desmond died a tragic death? It explains his message of love. Perhaps he was unable to love in the end. And Desmond felt there was no reason to live without love."

Edward set tea on the table. He poured some for Gina and Lily. "I think that now Desmond will feel at peace. We understand his message."

A curtain gently fluttered at the window. A scent of vanilla wafted about the room. Edward poured tea for himself and Tilly. "We have other news."

"We will be leaving you for a bit. We are going to take the Orient Express Train. We will travel from London to Istanbul," Tilly said excitedly.

Edward nodded. "And in between we will visit Paris, Lausanne, Milan, Venice, Belgrade, and Sofia."

"Gina, like the movie, *Murder on the Orient Express*! Do you remember?" Lily asked.

"Yes, I remember. The trip will be fantastic! But, we will miss you," Gina said.

"Go while you are young! Travel! Go! Live!" Edward and Tilly beamed at her and Lily.

"We have many people inside of us. You must pay attention to each of them," Tilly added. She kissed Gina's cheek.

40

School finished for the year. Without Sharie and Phil, the picnic wasn't as much fun. Gina and Tim spoke rarely. They only talked when he needed to leave patrol service early for baseball practice.

Gina rode the bus home from Minnehaha Falls with Danny. "Danny, the best thing about the picnic this year was you! Your illusions were the best!"

"I did have a great assistant," he smiled. Harry Houdini sat in his carrier between them. He petted Harry through the wires of his cage. Harry calmly munched a carrot.

Gina petted Harry, too. "Thank you. But, the new rope tricks were fantastic. No one had any idea how you cut them with a scissors and magically put them back together. And Harry did a ter-rific job. He only escaped twice!"

"Too bad you won't have time to do birthday parties this summer. You'll be in ballet class all day, right?" Danny asked.

Gina thought for a moment. "No. I'm not going to ballet classes. I can't do it. I don't want to talk about it."

Danny frowned. "Maybe think some more about that."

The bus pulled up to the school. Gina helped Danny get Harry Houdini and his illusion stuff home. "Bye, Danny. Let me know when you need help with birthday parties!"

"Will do. Take it easy. And think about going to ballet class!" he insisted.

Gina waved as she made her way to the side-walk. The weather was beautiful and warm. Trees and flowers were blooming everywhere. "I'm not sneezing! Dr. Halverson's shots are working!"

She skipped a little. "I shouldn't skip. Should I? Seventh grade next year!" she thought.

She caught her bus home. Gina walked into the dining room. "Hi, mom."

Lily was filling out forms at the table. "I'm reg-istering you for summer ballet."

"Mom, I just can't," Gina said.

Lily looked up. "Gina, are you sure?"

"Yes, I don't want to dance!" Gina said firmly.

Lily sighed. "It's okay. I will call Madame."

Gina stayed close. She heard Madame say to Lily on the phone, "Gina will be back. I will wait."

After Lily hung up the phone Gina said, "I'm sorry, mom."

Lily put an arm around Gina. "You are doing what you need to do. It's good! Please let Danny know the Pride Parade is coming up."

"He's excited about going." Gina ate a cookie. "No more homework for three whole months!"

The day of the Pride Parade arrived. Gina awakened. She went downstairs. Lily was in the living room. "Mom, its Pride today! Danny's brother is driving him over here."

"Pride is today?" Lily looked confused for a second.

"Yes! Let's get ready. Danny will be here soon." Gina thought, "How could mom forget about Pride? She must have been thinking about something else. Maybe choreography she's working on."

Lily and Gina rode the bus to the Pride Parade as they had done last year. This time Danny joined them.

"Danny, I wasn't sure you would be interested in Pride," Lily commented. The bus rolled along.

"Anything that has a party for people who are different? I'm in!" Danny declared.

They soon reached Loring Park. Lily's friend, Ben, was at the bus stop, waiting for them. "Fifteen thousand people are expected this year," Ben announced. They found a table and Ben poured lemonade.

They looked around at the crowds. Many wore tee shirts. *Rightfully Proud* and *Look to the Future* was printed on them. Music was playing. People were dancing. Old and young, people danced with each other, with strangers, with family.

"Great things happen when people are having a picnic," Gina said.

Lily rose to dance. "And dancing."

"What do you mean great things happen?" Danny asked.

Gina answered, "That picnic on the border between Austria and Hungary. That picnic started the Berlin Wall coming down. All the Pride picnics have started people being kind to each other."

"And don't forget. John Lennon met Paul McCartney at a church picnic in Liverpool. From that picnic we got the Beatles and their fantastic music!" Ben added.

Lily announced, "Oh, I forgot to tell you! Gene is moving home! He'll live in Northfield and teach at Carlton University. He's their new Russian professor."

"How far away is Northfield?" Gina wondered.

"You can drive there in an hour," Danny said.

"Fantastic!" Gina grabbed Danny's hand. "Let's dance!"

Danny smiled. "I thought you gave up dancing," he laughed.

Gina twirled Danny. "Everyone here helps me feel like all that matters is dance!"

"And just to love," Danny reminded her.

"That, too," Gina agreed.

It was a long, wonderful day of music, dancing, and picnicking. They saw old friends and made new ones. The four set off for home. Ben and Danny were staying for dinner. They entered the house. Edward was in the dining room.

"We would have gone with you to the picnic, but it's quite hot out today," Edward remarked. He set a platter of grilled chicken and burgers on the table.

Tilly came in with a large salad and rolls. "Edward is a delicate flower. He melts in the sun!" She set everything down. "We thought we would have dinner ready when you arrived instead. To keep the party going!"

"Thank you for doing all of this!" Lily said.

"And there is strawberry shortcake for dessert!" Edward rubbed his hands together. "I'll whip the cream when we are ready. Please sit!"

All sat and enjoyed the delicious dinner. The phone rang. Lily rose. "I'll get it."

She answered the phone in the kitchen. "Yes, Madame. Yes, she missed the beginning of summer classes this year. I'm sure you know, she was upset about leaving the recital. I will tell her. Thank you, Madame. You are very kind. Good Bye."

Lily returned to the dining room.

Gina looked up anxiously. "That was Madame?"

"Yes! Madame Branitskaya has spoken!" Lily imitated Madame's Ukrainian accent, "Enough! Gina comes to ballet class on Monday! Early to work hard!"

Danny asked, "Gina, will you go back?"

Everyone around the table looked at Gina. They waited for her answer.

Gina thought for a moment. Then she said, "I got sick at the recital. But I didn't wreck anything forever. I sort of spent the year dancing backwards."

"And?" Danny pressed.

Gina took a breath. "I'll go to ballet class. And dance forwards this time!"

Everyone clapped. "Well done! An excellent decision! I knew you'd change your mind!" was all Gina heard.

"I'll call Madame right back!" Lily rushed to the phone. "Yes, Madame. She will be there! Oh, yes. We will buy pointe shoes in the morning."

The party continued. The strawberry short-cake was scrumptious. Edward insisted on serving it. He made little figures in whipped cream on Gina's and Danny's pieces. Gina's had a tiny pointe shoe. Danny's had his initials "DM."

As Eddie put on the whipped cream, Danny asked "Can you please put my middle name on mine? I love whipped cream."

Edward smiled. He set the bowl of whipped cream near him. "Write out all of *War and Peace* if you like."

"*War and Peace*?" Danny asked. He grabbed the spoon. He began putting a mountain of whipped cream on his shortcake.

"It's a really long book. My uncle has probably read it," Gina answered. "And give me the spoon when you're done!"

After everyone was gone and the dishes were done, Gina and Lily went upstairs.

"It was a great day, mom. Am I really getting pointe shoes tomorrow?"

"Yes! I will show you how to sew the ribbons. Sweet dreams."

"You, too!"

Later in bed, Gina turned over. She cuddled Nijinsky and drifted off to sleep. She dreamed of flowing chiffon and pointe shoes. In the dream, she was in a dusty backstage wing. She listened to the sound of an orchestra tuning up. In her sleep, Gina smiled. Like a fluttering ribbon, ballet was stirring.

The End

EXCERPT FROM GRAND JETÉ
(THE FIRST BOOK IN
THE BALLET SERIES)

Her uncle's house felt cold to Gina, and damp. She rounded the corner on the walk home from school and shivered looking at it. Uncle Eugene's white and grey house was three stories tall with gardens surrounded by a curling black iron fence. It was two hour's drive from her old house in Minneapolis. Her uncle's house in Northfield might as well have been on another planet. Gina sighed and took the mail out of the box. She unlocked the heavy door with her key.

She looked at herself for a moment in the mirror on the closet door as she hung up her coat. Gina was twelve and a half. She was dark-haired, small, and slender like her mother had been. Born to dance, she had heard people say.

Gina shut the closet door. She didn't take off her navy uniform sweater. It was late February of 1991. Although it was growing warmer everyday, it was winter in Minnesota. The afternoon had a dark early evening feeling. She hugged her arms to herself.

Her gaze shifted to the open curving staircase and she watched for her cat, Nijinsky, to come out. Gina walked on polished wooden floors through large beautiful rooms with graceful furniture to the kitchen. Everything was neatly arranged according to her Uncle Gene's wishes. No soft mounds of clothes were strewn about. There was not a single strain of music to stir up painful memories of her mother.

Nijinsky appeared and brushed his grey-striped face against her ankles. She missed Nijinsky all day at school.

Having hugged Nijinsky, Gina put him down to sit by her ankles. Out of deep green eyes she looked at the mail. There was nothing from her father. There never was.

He had left Gina and her mother when Gina was eight. She remembered hearing her mother arguing with him when he was drunk. Even so, Gina looked for him at her mother's funeral. He never appeared.

A week after her mother's funeral Gina came to Northfield to live with her Uncle Eugene. Gina left her old school, her old home, and ballet lessons behind. She was miserably forced to attend St. Elizabeth's Middle School near her uncle's house.

She looked at the notice of parent-teacher conferences from St. Elizabeth's that was in the mail. Today at school hadn't been quite so awful, she thought. Considering it was only slightly less awful than the day before.

Gina thought of the girls at school this morning. A smug girl, surrounded by a pack of her horrid friends, had come up to Gina at her locker.

The snobby girl asked, "Is it true that your mother died of cancer?"

"What? What do you know about my mother?" asked Gina in surprise.

"Oh, Mrs. Murdock told us to be nice to you because your mother died." The girls stood around and waited for Gina to answer.

"Mrs. Murdock! She said that to you!?" Gina stepped back in shock.

"What kind of cancer was it, anyway? Are you afraid you'll get cancer someday?" one of the other girls pressed.

"That's none of your business!" Gina shot back.

"I only ask because if there are other students like you here, maybe I could get up a little grief club. I'm president of the eighth grade. It's my duty to see that our student body is well-served."

"Leave me alone!" Gina almost shouted.

Gina wanted to punch her. It would have hurt, too, with those braces on her teeth. Gina chose instead to loudly slam her locker door. She gave her long, dark hair a toss and walked away. She heard the voices of the girls behind her, "Can you believe that? I was just trying to be nice."

Gina set the mail down on her uncle's kitchen counter with a similar slam. She hugged Nijinsky again. She fed him his dinner. He liked only dry, crunchy cat food, day in and day out. Yesterday her Uncle Gene brought home liver, shrimp, and lobster-flavored treats to entice Nijinsky. Gina knew from the excitement in his voice when he called for Nijinsky, that he had a new brand of kitty treat. Then she heard his sigh as Nijinsky gave one sniff and turned away in revulsion

Her uncle, Dr. Eugene Shostek, was a professor in the Russian Studies department at Carlton College. He was tall, dark-haired, and starting to grey. At forty-five years old, he was handsome and youthful. Dr. Shostek, was known as "Gene" to family and friends. He had sparkling charm and a kind heart.

Gene had visited Russia many times to work or to study. Russia is often called "The Land of Ballet" and Gene had gone many times to see beautiful ballet performances when he was there. His sister, Lily, was Gina's mom. Lily asked Gene to take of Gina when she knew she was dying.

In the kitchen at Gene's house the phone rang. Gina picked it up, hearing Uncle Gene's voice.

"Yes, Uncle Gene, I got in just fine. I answered the phone didn't I?"

"Yes, Nijinsky is fine, too."

"No, the stove is not on."

"Uncle Gene, you ask me the same stuff every day!"

"Yes, I'll do my homework. I love you, too. Bye." Gina replaced the receiver. Gina knew her uncle worked late because he loved being a professor of Russian. So much that he wanted her to learn the Russian language, too!

Last Sunday evening, Gene sat Gina down in the dining room to teach her the Russian alphabet. Gina could hear the seconds ticking away from the grandfather clock in the hall. Gina found Russian monstrously confusing. She gazed politely at the books Gene placed in front of her. All the while she planned her escape. She finally burst out, "Uncle Gene, I don't need to know the Russian alphabet!"

"But it would be excellent for you to know it!" Patiently she listened to his *Learn the Russian Alphabet* lecture that he gave to university students. "Two little old monks, Cyril and Methodius sat down one day and wrote the Russian alphabet. Isn't that fascinating?"

"Fascinating? Are you kidding?" Gina looked at him in disbelief.

"It's not as foreign as you think. Look at these letters, Gina, you already know them."

She looked over the letters, "A, Z, K, M, O, T." He crowed, "There you've already knocked off six of them!"

"Uncle Gene, there are twenty eight more letters. The Russian C is an S, P is an R, and H is an N. That's not even counting the letters that don't even look like letters!" she pleaded. She pointed to the alphabet in front of her. "See that! That's a squiggle!"

"Gina, my dear, some day I know you will thank me for teaching you the Russian language. We might travel on the Trans-Siberian railway together in winter! And you will become a Russian ballerina! How delightful!"

"Uncle Gene, I will not eat borscht and wear woolen scarves on my head! No way! And no more ballet!" Gina shuddered at the thought.

He ignored her and went on. "Learn this letter with a picture. For example, look at the letter X. It makes a harsh 'H' sound, right? So if you imagine a pair of HOCKEY sticks crossed in an X, you'll remember the sound 'H!'" He had removed his suit coat and tie at this point.

"But, Uncle Gene, what if I remember HUBCAP instead of HOCKEY sticks and end up with an O instead of an X?" She begged off to go to her room. Gene sadly put the books away as Gina disappeared down the hall.

She sat down on her new bed in her uncle's house. Gina had loved her mother's funny old house in Minneapolis. It had been built in the year 1910 and was forever falling apart. The doors and staircases creaked, doorknobs fell off in their hands, and the faucets leaked. Gina and her mother were sure the place was haunted. Gina had loved all of its nooks and crannies and messes and joy.

Mostly she missed her mother, Lily. Her mother was a ballet teacher. She taught Gina her very first steps. Gina got up from her bed. She looked into the mirror above the dresser. She made slow graceful, movements with her arms.

When Gina was four years old she began dancing in the mirror after she saw ballet dancers on television. By the time she was eight years old she loved to listen to Debussy's *L' Apres Midi d' Un Faun*. It was so beautiful it made her cry. Gina knew there was something delicate and graceful about herself.

She picked up her pink satin pointe shoes from the dresser and held them. In Minneapolis Gina had loved pointe shoes, ballet lessons, and her teacher, Madame Branitskaya, who was from Russia. Gina lay back on the bed, staring at the ceiling, picturing her mother in her mind. She re-membered Lily's voice from one of the last times she was with her in the hospital.

"Gina, did you practice your dancing?" Lily had asked sitting up in bed.

"Of course, I did mom. Watch this!" Gina had learned a new step. She executed a springy "pas de basque" perfectly for her mom.

"Gina, that is wonderful!" she remembered Lily exclaiming in delight.

Gina slowly put her pointe shoes back into their pink, mesh bag and set them back on the dresser. For two long months, since moving in with her uncle, she hadn't danced at all. She didn't have the heart to practice. Gina felt too sad. Her heart was empty and she hurt. She would never hear Lily's voice again.

She sat down on the floor. She hated crying, but she couldn't seem to stop herself. She tried to cry quietly so that her Uncle Gene wouldn't hear her. She hated it even more when he came in and tried to comfort her. She heard a soft knock at the door.

"Uncle Gene, I'm okay," she sniffled, getting tissues from the dresser.

"Would you like to like to watch the news with me?" he gently asked.

"I'm really okay. I'm going to bed." She blew her nose.

"All right, dear Gina. Sweet dreams."

"You, too, Uncle Gene."

She put on her nightgown and climbed into bed. Gina burrowed her head into her pillow. She remembered her first recital for Madame Branit-skaya. She had been sick to her stomach and ran away from the theater.

"I don't have enough courage to dance in the theater, anyway. It's a good thing I quit," she said to herself. Gina found herself talking to the ceiling, "Mom, you used to promise me you would teach me how to get over stage fright. Now you're gone and it's too late! Anyway, no one cares if I dance or not. Even if I did, they wouldn't like it."

Gina turned her radio on to the classical station with the volume on very low. Even if Uncle Gene heard the radio, she knew he wouldn't mind her listening to classical music. A piece of music was playing that her mother had danced to, the music by Tchaikovsky for *The Russian Dance* in the *Nutcracker Fantasy* ballet.

Gina thought that she would never be able to perform on stage the beautiful way her mother had. Gina loved to watch her mother do the simplest things, like walking. There was something so breathlessly delicate and powerful about Lily's walk.

"I miss you, mom." Gina turned over and tried to go to sleep.

READ THE REST
OF GRAND JETÉ

Grand Jeté

*In grief over her mother's death,
twelve year-old Gina vows never to dance ballet again.*

Young Gina oddly feels a ghostly love and encouragement from her mother, Lily, to dance.

Gina leaves her childhood home to live with the only family left to care for her, Uncle Gene.

Uncle and niece move to Leningrad, home of the famous Kirov Ballet Academy.

As tensions rise in the city and Russia nearly breaks apart, Gina desperately tries to overcome stage fright. She tries to enjoy dancing once again with the help of her new friends.

On the day that President Gorbachev is arrested, the city erupts in panic and Gina becomes lost in crowds of people.

Will her uncle find her? Will she ever see her Russian friends again?   Can she dance without their help?

Grab it today!
https://www.albertsbridgebooks.com

JOIN THE NEWSLETTER

Keep in touch about all the books at Albert's Bridge books ... plus occasional deals on other mysteries! And no spam!

Go to https://www.albertsbridgebooks.com to join!

ABOUT THE AUTHOR

Amy Shomshak studied Russian and ballet during many travels to Russia. She has an M.Ed. in Kinesiology from the University of Minnesota.

She lives in Minneapolis with her husband, two greyhounds and three cats.